MW01701311

Farm to Foul Play

CAPITOL CRIMES

2024 Anthology

Foreword by Tori Eldridge

Edited by Jennifer K. Morita

ISBN: 978-1-7369391-3-0

Farm to Foul Play is an anthology of fiction. While some locations desribed are real places and, on occasion, historical figures may be referenced, the stories told and the characters who populate them are the product of the authors' imaginations.

Cover design and formatting by Karen Phillips, PhillipsCovers.com

Published by Capitol Crimes, the Sacramento, California Chapter
of Sisters in Crime.
CapitolCrimes.org

This anthology is dedicated to Capitol Crimes founding member Pat Canterbury, who continues to champion Sacramento area crime writers while promoting literacy for our region's youngest readers.

Contents

Foreword

Tori Eldridge

It was such a pleasure to be asked to write the foreword for *Farm to Foul Play,* not only because of my love for the Capitol Crimes chapter of Sisters in Crime, but because of the Sacramento Valley agricultural theme. Whether it's a town, ethnicity, or family, so much of a community's culture is revealed through the crops we grow, the methods we use, and the cherished recipes they inspire. It's hard to imagine home without the warm remembrance of family recipes and favorite foods. Whether its biscuits and gravy, sopa de papa, congee, or butterfish-pork laulau dipped in two-day-old poi—one of my faves—if you want to understand a community, home cooking and agriculture is often the best place to begin.

Not only do the mouth-watering additions give a more visceral experience to readers, the types of food and the agricultural settings help to convey a deeper understanding and visualization of place. In my new mystery novel, *Kaua'i Storm,* I was able to establish the culture, identity, and personality of my ranger protagonist and her homesteading grandmother by staging their conversation in a taro paddy, thigh-deep in mud. I noticed similar cultural integrations in the short stories presented in *Farm to Foul Play.*

Much can be learned about a community through its farming methods and crops. But to avoid superfluous descriptions, the trick is to include details that reveal character and drive the scene.

The stories in *Farm to Foul Play* capture the agricultural community of the Sacramento Valley in similar ways by illuminating the community's culture, defining the setting, and driving the plots. From tomatoes to chickens to ranching, each of these stories plays on the same agricultural theme. At the same time, readers will enjoy a variety of genres from quaint and cozy to sinister and grim.

Each of the fifteen contributing members of Capitol Crimes digs beyond the expectation one might have of California's capital to discover Sacramento's idiosyncrasies and rural charm. One can hardly pen a story set in Sacramento without at least a nod to agriculture: California's Central Valley produces a quarter of our nation's food supply and forty percent of our fruits and nuts. It's inextricably entwined with the farming and ranching industries on which its economy thrives and survives. Or as Virginia V. Kidd's protagonist says more quaintly in her story, "Farm to Fingers," Sacramento is the "Farm-to-Fork capital, you know."

I enjoy reading and writing stories that introduce me to new cultures or deepen my understanding of places and peoples already familiar to me. The local details paint a picture in my mind, awaken my senses, and root me in that specific time and locale. But the setting becomes more than a backdrop in a story with a distinctive cultural voice. It reflects the personality of the characters and the piece as a whole.

Every story in the *Farm to Foul Play* anthology has a bold and distinct voice. Whether it's the unexpectedly insightful small-town detective in "Death of an Ugly Woman," by William Bishop, or the hen-pecked husband of a wannabe-chicken farmer in "Mother Clucker," by Sarah Bresniker, or the sinister second-person point of view rancher in "Half a Heart," by Brian Shea, each of the fifteen contributing authors tells their tale with a unique and entertaining flair.

Several of the cozier stories feature young, inquisitive protagonists as in "The Sacramento Truck Farm," by Elaine Faber, in which a Nancy Drew fan in the 1920s tries to solve a string of robberies from her family's fruit stand, or when the college-bound rural sleuth in Karen A. Phillips' mystery stirs up neighborhood trouble while investigating "The Case of the Naked Scarecrow." For a fun twist, Linda Joy Singleton pairs a disgruntled teen and her semi-delinquent brother in "Fowl Play" to find their grandma's missing prize Swedish Black chicks. The family elements of these stories capture the rural community feel.

Other stories in *Farm to Foul Play* dive into the high-drama world of Sacramento's celebrated farm-to-fork cuisine. In "Dear John Deere," Chris Dreith weaves in an actual high-ticketed fundraising event when her well-seasoned PIs follow a missing tractor to the annual Tower Bridge Dinner. Susan Egan sets her deadly mystery during a fiction contest in "The Competition," which takes place during Sacramento's annual Farm-to-Fork Festival. Emotions heat up as she pits a spurned lover against her ex-fiancé.

Also in the culinary vein, Dänna Wilberg presents a quickly paced, multi-POV whodunnit to solve the murder of a celebrity chef of a restaurant that's re-opening after protests during the pandemic forced them to close. By integrating actual events in the not-too-distant past, she grounds her fiction in fact. On a more serious side, Darrell Smith integrates Black history into Sacramento's agricultural theme by having the ancestor of his protagonist be a Montford Point Marine during WWII as one of the US Marine Corps' first Black recruits before moving to Sacramento and purchasing his land. "Starkrimson" is set in contemporary times when "the land wars are fought in courtrooms. They don't burn crosses, they hire expensive Los Angeles lawyers dressed in Savile Row suits."

I really enjoy reading and writing stories and novels that not only weave facts into fiction but ground fiction into actual timelines, history, locations, and current events.

In *Farm to Foul Play,* Joanna Vander Vlugt makes it easy to visualize her cold case murder mystery, "The Lady in Pink," with her cinematic writing and use of actual locations like Estelle Bakery and Pâtisserie, and Avery Pond. Reading all fifteen stories in this anthology is like taking a trip through Sacramento Valley's lesser-known rural charm.

The variations between cozy and sinister are particularly fun. Karen Harrington's "Midtown Market Girl" packs a powerful punch. Debra Henry's "Winging It" is a crime fiction mystery that combines poignant emotions, drug-dealing danger, and scorching jalapeño wings. Nick Webster's "Fair and Fowl" lightens the mood when a pet detective is hired by an insurance agency to investigate a chicken theft during a 4-H livestock competition. And all of this is edited and arranged by Jennifer K. Morita to maximize reader experience and keep up the pace.

Have fun in Sacramento. You're in for an enjoyable ride!

HALF A HEART

Brian Shea

You did it for your Granda', you tell yourself, because you'd do anything for Granda'. Really, though, you did it for yourself.

From the very first time you saw the tall fellow that bought the Johnson place down below the ridge—from the way he waltzed across the property, thumbs hitched in the belt loops of his ironed jeans, from the way he kept at the bottle of that bright, blue sports drink, from even his vehicle, a glossy black Range Rover with tinted windows—you knew he was a thorn, and you would do something about him.

Had to.

***

The morning following the newcomer's arrival, you're up earlier than usual. After the feeding, but before walking the fence line looking for burrows or tangled critters, you set one foot up on an oak stump and pick a few blackberries. It's early enough, so the yellow jackets aren't organized for sugar patrol. The air wants to be cool, but the only coolness is trapped in dew drops, and they are shrinking as the kraken rays of the sun touch them.

The newcomer looks like one of those fancy fellows. Not gay. Anyway, you don't have a leaning one way or the other about that sort of thing. Let a man—or woman—be with whomever, though you wouldn't say that in front of your

Granda'. He's set in his ways about everything, from the way he makes coffee to the hour when he puts his tired feet up at the end of a day. The tall newcomer seems like one of those preacher-farmers, sustainable this, eco that, urging measures to conserve water, though that's most important to him since the water rights re-set to zero after Mr. Johnson abandoned the place. If you know the newcomer's type—and oh, you do—he talks to anyone and everyone about heirloom varieties of squash and whatnot, the same kind Granda' and his Da' ditched when higher yields were developed by smart kids and government men down at the ag school.

You vow you'll hold out, not introduce yourself to the newcomer. He has a bumper sticker on that fancy car that says "Locavore." Well, he'll find his own kind down in that crowd that shows up on the Capitol Mall, munching grass-fed this'es and that's, Equadoran fry-breads and bowls of crickets and such, done up every hour on the hour by fancy chefs wired to rock-star microphones.

Granda' says that food festival thing is kind of odd, scheduled for the hot, breezeless days of September. What sort of personal relationships with chefs and farmers do those people boast about, anyway, when they need a map to locate them at a festival?

Slow Food, now that's different. First names, no crowds. Six years—or seven, was it?—after you proved yourself working alongside Granda,' the other ranchers got to asking you to come and eat with them at a long table. You dressed up, for once. Maybe people noticed, and maybe they didn't. But you liked doing it.

The early October air, beaten and blistered all day, didn't hold the bitter burned iron of a summer evening. Perhaps there was an early down breeze from the Sierra, you don't recall exactly. Not a single soul preached about what to do or what not to do. Mostly, folks told jokes and laughed under string lights as night crept up like a lonely wool blanket. Nobody commented on the drop in temperature until they walked in a satisfied silence back to their Silverados and duallies.

You've been at Granda's side for more than ten years now. Ten years of stacking haybales over your head, pasture range dust and alfalfa splinters showering down into your hair and eyes. Ten years of topping off water troughs. Ten years of blisters. Ten years of barbed wire pecking at your knuckles. Ten years of slipping and falling in the muck that comes with icy, sideways rains in January. Ten years of bliss.

Until that Range Rover fellow shows up down the way. The man's smile is like a hug you need, yet he makes you uncomfortable.

Some afternoons, he's down there waving his arms like a drowning person. Stands on his toes, as if that'll send his greeting farther. You stare away into the late-day sun, basking in the solar gilt that skims over grasses and splashes off barns, ranch houses and crumpled old sheds, briefly making them siblings of the Tower Bridge downtown. Your distraction lets you pretend to be oblivious to the man below the ridge flailing his arms and calling out, "Hello, I'm Charlie!" He could be from Vermont, for all you know, or from San Francisco or Santa Cruz. One thing you're sure of: he's a "loca-bore," as you call people in that crowd.

Most days, however, the black Range Rover is gone. Maybe Charlie takes that winsome smile of his and gets out to cattle auctions, though you doubt it. He doesn't have a rig to move livestock. He could be doing breed research down at the ag school—or, more likely, soil testing at the master gardener's office over at the Placer County courthouse.

You think, what kind of ranch owner isn't at his ranch, drinking in the dust and holding down the thirst of work?

The Johnson place went unkempt, like hat hair. When spring's purple vetch tires, rumpled sedges and pockets of melic grass encroach, and later, Idaho fescue and the dark burgundy pompadours of curly dock join the melee. Thistles are the final summer insult, ornery, stubborn and defended with daggers. It's gonna be tough to graze again at the Johnson place.

Your ranch has been in the family since before California was a state. The stagecoach rattling up to Carson City used to load up nearby, and although nobody knows exactly where the stop was, they all have their stories, and parts of those stories, you reason, must be right. Your family spread is a legacy, nesting well above where the Sacramento and San Joaquin waterways confer in summer and convey flooding in winter. The lower delta, emptied of failed settlers, is reserved now as a destination touristed by waterfowl like egrets and ducks and sandhill cranes who come at the end of the season shrieking at the blackbirds and crows and chasing away anything else in their temporary arena.

People reminisce with stories about Granda' and you but skip what's between. Your Da' had some kind of wild in him and wanted to try skydiving. When you were four, he and your mother drove to Kansas, where one of his college friends crop-dusted and towed kids up to jump. Parachute packing was treated as a casual affair, which proved to be fatal for your parents. Granda' took you in as his own daughter. People don't shy from tragedy, but it's another story when a young girl's involved.

In the chilly months after harvest—and after the food festivals pack it in—you drive into the city to do face-to-faces with the restaurant men who buy your butchered animals. The connections are Granda's. In the old boys' club, he's a natural, sitting and trading jokes over a cold beer before any talk of buying and selling can surface. You try to be like him. But the club doesn't know how to treat a woman.

You negotiate future orders in the city, but conversations soon shift to gossip about the new fellow. "Forgettin' his name," says Smitty at Harpo's, "but some fellow come in askin' after you. Nice fellow. Always drinkin' some colored drink he had with him." At another stop, Mamie, covered in sailor's tattoos, says, "Must be fixin' to plant his feet here. Yessir, that boy got some ambition, he does."

Charlie, an old boy already?

You drive back in evening light that's reluctant to surrender as if it feels guilt over not bringing enough heat. You storm in your truck. Charlie, with his grin and bottled blue drink, is trying to push you and Granda' out, cheat in on your family legacy. Charlie probably told those restaurant men they'd be able to double their prices using his fancy products on their menus. Restaurants won't turn that down in this economy. "Damn him!" The windshield shudders.

Not all men are disagreeable, you tell yourself, but with only half a heart. The man who butchers your cattle and sheep treats you fair. He brings the mobile slaughter rig, the one the USDA makes small ranchers use if they don't want to drive a hundred miles to some big operation in the valley. The government man don't mind if you fatten up your animals on corn, and he don't tell you what to do on your own spread. He smokes a hand-rolled, squints against the reflection off the stainless rig, and asks how you're faring. And he'll ask after Granda', whom he calls James Jr. The government man cuts your animals clean, has a smoke and a chat, and that's that. No fancy smiles.

Charlie's not easy like that. A signal oozes out from him. Charlie is on your mind, so he's too close. You have to take Charlie out of the equation.

You're curious, though, why the light in Mrs. Johnson's kitchen stays on until very late. You don't believe in ghosts. But the kitchen is suspicious.

When you were 20, Granda' told you to take Mrs. Johnson a casserole. You both knew it wouldn't help save her from breast cancer. "We do it anyway," Granda' told you. The Johnson farm went empty afterward. The casserole dish probably still lies in that kitchen, but neither you nor Granda' want it back. Besides, it's probably stained blue from Charlie's sports drink. You want nothing from that kitchen and nothing from the newcomer who lives there.

As you sit on the porch in the dark, the gleam from the barrel of your .223 gets you thinking. The rifle? Too obvious. Or cutting the brake line of his fancy car? Probably has an alarm that would wake the dead. In your mind, you paste together a threatening note, but what would the threat be? How about a fire in his barn? It could spread to your family's spread. Everyone has Roundup nowadays. Gastro corrosion would be fatal, but how to get someone to ingest that much? There's always strychnine and cyanide—you've read a few mystery books. Yet nothing calls out to you.

You go to bed angry and restless.

The next day, you start on off-season chores, clean out an old shed at the far end of the property where hornets tussle with each other for a sliver of shade by the overhang. After batting away the spider webs, your eye goes to a high shelf. Blue fluid with a worn label.

Paraquat.

Charlie still feels like a threat, but your restlessness wanes and lets your shoulders drop, finally.

You wait for one of those days when the sun tricks people into thinking it's hotter than it really is. You drive down and see Charlie on his porch, fanning himself with a new River Cats cap. Your boot heels clomp across the cattle guard and you open his gate.

He stops fanning. Stands. "Well, well."

You crook your head, reminding yourself not to reveal your irritation. When you're close, you say, "No livestock?"

"Hoping for some goats," he says. He folds and refolds the bill of his cap.

Went right to skirting talk about cattle, you notice. "I should say hello. I'm Vicky. I'm up there with the old guy." You point to where you come from.

"You're with *him*?" His smile drips with mischief.

"Not *with* him, no. Oh. You didn't think—" You stop, realize you missed his humor.

"Just teasing. I'm Charlie. But you know that. I've called out to you a hundred times."

Damn him. His smile is more inviting than the other men you encounter. Way more. Tempting, even. "Here," you say. You twist off the cap and hold your hand out with a blue sports drink. "I think you like this stuff."

"Great. I'm so dehydrated." His smile.

"Shoulda been here last August." Your own smile is literally painful, like a snag of barbed wire across your palm.

He stands, takes the bottle. "I'll get some glasses."

You wave your arms, make a sour face. "Can't stand the stuff. Gotta go, anyhow. A culvert needs clearing." You take a step back, away from him and the blue drink.

His smile drops, but his voice is still hopeful. "See you again soon, I hope?"

You walk away, trying to outrun your nerves. Out the gate. Bang across the cattle guard. To home, where there are no smiles.

***

Next month you're in the city again. More meetings. You're there to secure the restaurants you may have lost.

Afterwards, you look for an excuse to delay the drive so you can enjoy the humps of the Sutter Buttes through a sunset haze. Granda' will be asleep. You treat yourself to dinner. While a steak cooks, the waiter brings you a goblet and a bottle of a red blend.

"This one's new," he says. "We're lucky to have it. This guy, he blends it in his house, he told me. Just 35 cases." The waiter gushes out a generous taste. "Hasn't come back with the second case we ordered, though." He steps back and looks for your approval.

The wine's alive. It calls out like love.

You reach for the bottle. The label says "Vicky."

And in small, unpretentious lettering is the name of the neighbor you killed.

MOTHER CLUCKER

Sarah Bresniker

Of course, it was the chickens. It was always the chickens. Rosie loved the scruffy balls of feathers, but I agreed with Pops. They were dumb as rocks and would eat their young if you let them. He'd been the thirteenth of thirteen kids raised on a chicken ranch, so he knew the worst side of the little buggers. Had the worst jobs he loved to tell us kids about, and once he left that ranch, he never let a bite of chicken pass his lips again. He certainly never let them wander through his house wearing skirts.

But Rosie? She thinks they're cute. Wants eggs with no processing or antibiotics or something. And she's cute, and knows all the right things to say to turn me into a pool of butter, so we got the chickens. Pops would roll over if he saw it. If he knew I'd built a fancy chicken coop with windows, windows with real glass and tiny flower boxes, even a miniature chandelier, I'd never hear the end of it. But that's how it goes. We all make choices, some better than others.

I thought lately I was making some good choices, but you know that never lasts. That tiny chandelier cost more than any light I'd ever seen. And the feed, and then some complicated water mister thing for when it got too hot for the chickens. I'm pretty sure Pops just used a hose. Or let them sweat if that's something chickens do. The old ranch is just a few miles away, in Orangevale, but Rosie's girls, as she calls them, live in a different universe than Pop's mangy stew hens did.

Then there's the garden. We're just renting; no way we could own something like this, and the yard is a postage stamp. But Rosie wanted a garden, organic vegetables without chemicals, just like the eggs. Who knows how much each of the carrots she grew actually cost us, with the tools, the sprays and the special dirt that looked like regular old dirt to me. I have to admit, though, they did taste better than the ones you could buy at Walmart. But still not as good as a burger.

So, when Tank came around with an idea, it was just polite to listen. Maybe he's not a whole lot smarter than a chicken, but he's more convincing. He knew a guy who knew a guy. Easy money and I liked the sound of that. I made sure he only came around when Rosie was at work at the hospital. She wasn't a fan. Not a fan of any of my friends, if I think back. Maybe that should have been a sign. But like I said, butter. The girl knew how to speak my language when she wanted to.

Tank and I would hang out, drink a few beers, make our plans. In case you were wondering, there are no Alanis Morissette fans in his family. Tank's a tank, basically was the whole O-line in high school, and his dog Tiny is a teacup terrier. I told him he needed to keep that little terror on a leash, but neither one of them liked to listen. They showed up one day and Tiny bolted out of Tank's truck and straight for the chicken coop before I could even shout. Yipping the whole way, he flew across the yard and flung himself at the wire mesh protecting the precious hens from predators. Coyotes, raccoons, and Tiny. His claws stuck in the mesh about five feet in the air, and he hung there, shaking and yipping, a fuzzy spider I was dying to swat. I cracked up, but Tank didn't. Oh, and did you know that the mesh I had to put up, dug down nearly a foot to make sure nothing could sneak underneath and put not just around the coop but over it too? It's not chicken wire. No sir. That's not safe for today's chickens.

They need hardware cloth. Smaller holes between the wire and more expensive, of course.

Tank ran and rescued Tiny, moaning and groaning, comforting the little mutt in a baby voice I couldn't believe belonged to him. I was laughing so hard I didn't even notice all the feathers flying everywhere. Where there's chickens, there's feathers.

But when Rosie got home, she noticed right away. "What did you do?" she asked like it had to be something I did. But I couldn't tell her Tank and Tiny were here. She'd lose it for sure, so I kept quiet. And she ran around the yard yelling, calling out to the hens like they knew their names. Now that I really looked, there were more feathers in the pen than usual and only one hen. Adele, I think. The really dumb one. She was standing with her head stuck in one of the openings in the trellis under the coop, and she wouldn't move no matter how hard Rosie tried to lure her out with mealworms and blueberries. Turns out the other two were in their egg boxes, and they weren't budging.

"Something happened," Rosie insisted. She wouldn't shut up about it. "How long was poor Adele standing there?"

Tank had left hours ago, but it wasn't on me that the hen was too stupid to take her head out of the hole once Tiny was gone. So, I played dumb like the chickens and just shrugged. But I could feel her looking at me differently, and that night, she didn't speak my language, just rolled over and put her eye mask on.

Maybe I should have tried to be nicer after that, but I was under a lot of stress. Tank's idea had potential but had issues too. Some we didn't realize until it was too late. And Rosie spent most of the time she was home out in the yard, even when it was over 100 degrees out. Cooing at those hens, talking to her garden. She added a tiny little weather vane on top of the coop, to go along with the chandelier, I guess.

A weather vane. With a teeny whale on top made out of tin. Like those hens were some fancy ladies living out on the East Coast, needing to know which way the wind was blowing their sailor husbands, back home or out to sea. You can find anything online these days, and none of it is cheap.

When she wasn't working or talking to the birds and the plants, she was going to chicken meetings. Meetings! About chickens! I didn't believe her at first, figured there had to be another guy, but sure enough. I followed her one night, and she pulled up at the library and spent two hours hanging out with a scraggly group of old dudes with uncombed beards and ladies with no makeup and long skirts. No threats there but a crazy way to waste her time.

And Tank and I were busy. We had a system and were bringing in some decent cash, but nothing lasts forever. Somebody always has to do something stupid, and sure enough, several people were stupid on the same day and I ended up with a dead body in the trunk of my car. I had to take it because there was no way to hide a body in Tank's truck. Seems like a choice he made on purpose, looking back on it. Rosie was working nights at the time, so we ditched Tank's truck down the road and pulled into the garage in my mom's old Buick. Tank always teased me about my old lady car, but he was glad to have it that day.

Once we were safe in the garage, Tank fixated on the giant chest freezer the previous tenant had left behind. He opened it and stuck his head down inside. "What is this stuff? Dead bugs?"

The only things we kept in that freezer were a few buckets of extra food for the chickens. "Dead bugs and worms. I'm not sure what else. Those stupid birds eat anything. The grosser the better."

"Anything?" Tank was running high on adrenaline and who knows what else.

"That's what my Pops always said. This stuff is disgusting. I won't let Rosie keep it in the house, but she hates this giant thing. She practically falls in every time she tries to get the food out."

"Well, what if we do a little project tonight?" I wasn't sure what he meant. "Make a platform type thing, so she doesn't have to reach way down in there. Just to help her out. Since you're such a loving boyfriend."

I peered into the freezer and thought. I had all of Pops' tools and lots of scraps from building the chicken coop. I was good at that kind of stuff.

"Yeah, I could do that. Wrap this guy up good and stick him underneath. Just for now, though. He can't stay here forever."

"No, no. Of course. And since you have the tools, it would be a lot easier to move him in pieces. Later."

I groaned but knew he was right. "As long as we have the saw going," I conceded, and we got to work. It was the middle of the night, but the neighbors knew better than to complain. They all had their own issues. We left each other to our own devices. I had built most of the coop in the wee hours after the bars closed. It was when I did my best work.

You wouldn't know it to look at him, but Tank is tidy. Likes things wiped down and in their place. Persnickety, even, Pops would have said. So, I worked the saw and the hammer, and he did the wrapping and wiping up. We were making good progress when the sky began lightening, and the hens started clucking. Not as bad as a rooster, but still annoying when the sun rises before six am.

"I bet you fifty dollars they don't eat everything," Tank said over the birds as he carefully wrapped the final arm.

I could see what he was thinking and didn't want any of it. "No, Tank. They're disgusting and so are you. And we need to finish up."

But he waggled the arm in my face, the fingers nearly scratching my nose. "Okay, a hundred. Chickens don't eat people. It doesn't make sense. People eat chickens." I could tell he wasn't going to stop, and I squeezed my eyes shut as he took the saw from me and made a quick chop. "Just a finger. I bet they run away as soon as they get a whiff."

But Tank was wrong. As the sun was coming up over the coop, he opened their gate and tossed the finger into their pen. And just like Pops said, those filthy hens were on it like bridesmaids fighting over a bouquet. Clucking and pecking, each wanting the treat all to herself. I couldn't watch. I went over to the back of the garage and lost what little was left in my stomach. I hadn't eaten anything since before the job and wasn't sure I'd ever eat again.

"Oh. My. God. You were right, Rex. But that was worth a hundred dollars. God, those birds are nasty."

"Clean it up," I moaned, not wanting to see any of it. "We need to be done. You need to be gone."

Tank went in to the pen and gathered up the finger bones while I went back to the garage. We got everything wrapped and tucked under the fancy shelf I'd made for the buckets of chicken feed. It looked good, I had to admit. I'd even slapped some baby blue paint on it before lowering it over the wrapped packages. Even if Rosie did look under, I could tell her we got some steaks, cheap. She wasn't eating meat now, so she'd just be annoyed.

When Tank finally left, I crashed. It had been a long day and a long night. And Tank hadn't even given me the hundred bucks.

***

I'm not sure how long I slept, but I was awakened by voices in the living room. Rosie, but I couldn't figure out who else. We didn't have a lot of company. Our friends never seemed to mix too well. I rolled over and tried to go back to sleep. Every muscle in my body was screaming from the effort of the night before. But the voices didn't stop, and finally, I realized I wouldn't get back to sleep without a piss. I lumbered out to the hall and toward the bathroom, but Rosie heard me.

"Rex? Is that you?"

"Yeah. Tired. Long night." I kept going toward the bathroom.

"This is Naomi from work. Come say hi."

I turned into the living room. The woman standing there with Rosie was someone I'd never seen or heard of before. No make-up, hair pulled back in a practical ponytail that puffed behind her head. No scrubs. She was wearing a gray blazer and black pants, even though it was already getting warm. She stood with her legs slightly apart, looking fit and ready to move at a moment's notice. Confident. Something that always turns me off in a woman.

"Hey."

"Naomi and I got to talking about chickens the other day. She's interested in getting her own. I've told her all about our girls. I wanted to show her how easy it is. And the coop. You did such a great job on it, Rex. It's so cute, I had to show it off." She would not stop talking and my head felt like a jack-hammer had taken residence in my skull.

"Great," I said and kept moving toward the bathroom.

"I love having chickens," she continued. "I wish I could have more, but the city limits us to three. Come out and see." They moved through the kitchen to the backyard. I couldn't believe she'd picked today to play chicken show-and-tell. But I didn't want to cause a scene, and I certainly didn't want to end up in a fight after this chick finally left. I didn't have the energy.

I could hear Rosie and her pal cooing over the dumb birds and the hens trilling in response. I checked myself in the mirror over the sink and broke into a cold sweat. Evidence of the night I'd had was all over me. One eye was swollen shut, and the side of my neck was scraped. At least that was kind of hidden by my tattoos. I splashed water on my face, winced at the sting, and tried to wake up. I needed to act normal.

Rosie was calling for me to come out to the yard. What could I do? I plastered on a smile as Naomi complimented my carpentry skills and Rosie taught her how to feed the birds. They were ravenous, and it took all I had not to be sick again.

"They really will eat anything," Rosie said. "But their favorite is worms. I'm thinking about starting a worm farm next. I saw how on YouTube. But for now, I just buy frozen ones. We have a big freezer in the garage." I turned away from them, hoping they didn't notice the blood draining out of my face.

"That's incredible," this new friend said, and I could feel her looking at me, rather than Rosie. "Rex, what do you think about the chickens? I bet you love the fresh eggs."

"Yeah, they're great," I said, pivoting back around. "Rosie is amazing with them. Spoils them rotten." She kept looking at me straight in the eye, just like that annoying Ms. Watson, the sixth-grade teacher I had who could always tell when I was lying. Then she casually pushed aside her blazer, revealing a holstered Glock and handcuffs secured to her belt. My knees nearly gave out as I stared back.

"Rex, I need you to put your hands up where I can see them." She'd unholstered the gun and pointed it at me before I even noticed. Was this some kind of kink?

"Rex, you're under arrest for the murder of Eric Smith. You have the right to remain silent. Anything you say can and will be used against you in a court of law. Do you understand?"

"Who's Eric Smith?" was all I could say, although I had an idea. "Who are you? I don't know what you're talking about!" Now I was mad, and the rage shooting through my body made it hard to hold still. But the gun pointed at my head was more persuasive. "Rosie, what the hell!"

As I said this, two uniformed officers came around the side of the garage. One grabbed my arms and cuffed them behind my back while the other trained his weapon on the target that was my skull. Once I was secured, Naomi lowered her Glock and pulled a tiny clear plastic bag out of her pocket. "Any idea what this is?"

I squinted as she held it up to my face. Inside was something small and whitish, curved and about the size of … Oh, Jesus, it looked like a fingernail: a whole one, not clippings. I didn't say anything as all of the adrenaline seeped from my body and left me even more exhausted than I'd been an hour ago.

"Apparently, these hens don't eat absolutely everything. I don't imagine they eat bones, either, do they, Rosie?" Rosie just shook her head, not meeting my eye. "And where was it you said you keep all of the frozen treats for these cuties? The garage?"

"You can't go in there." I could still put up a fight. I had rights. "You don't have a warrant."

But Rosie found her voice. "Rex, it's my name on the lease, remember. I'm the one who pays the rent check. You're supposed to pay half, but when is the last time that actually happened? This is my house. My garage. My chickens, my coop. Naomi, please make yourself at home."

Naomi cocked her head at the uniform who'd cuffed me and he strode to the garage. She didn't follow him, instead stepping closer to me. Right up next to me. "Officer Tanner will take a look if you don't mind, Rosie. I'd like to admire this coop you made, Rex, close up."

Had she lost her mind? Why did she care about the stupid coop? "Did you make this all yourself? Right here in the garage? I know some of the neighbors say you like to run that saw at all hours of the night. Not a great way to make friends, Rex."

"I made it—my contribution. Even if I can't always make the rent, Rosie, I help out. All the time."

Rosie laughed, a cold laugh I'd never heard from her before. She was always so sweet. Submissive. "Yeah, like forgetting to feed the chickens when you promised. Or never loading the dishwasher. Or scaring the chickens so bad they lost nearly all their feathers."

That last one hit, but I played dumb. "I don't know what you're talking about. Stupid birds are losing feathers all the time."

"Not all at once, Rex. Not unless something really scares them. And then they go hide and refuse to move. Stick their head somewhere to protect their neck. What did you do to them, Rex? What did they ever do to you?"

I couldn't help but grin, picturing Tiny clinging to the not chicken wire. It was funny. "What did they ever do? They're birds. Dirty, filthy rats with feathers. But you care more about them than about me. I'm your boyfriend. You owe me." I wanted to reach out, to shake her, but my hands were cuffed, and that second uniform still had his gun aimed at my head.

"Rex," Naomi butted in. "You should have been nicer to these sweet hens. They lay eggs for your breakfast. They're living creatures. But your own inability to be kind to your girlfriend's pets, could just be your downfall."

Now, I was confused and tried to make sense of the rest of the day. Why was this woman here? How had she found that fingernail? What had Rosie done? "You don't know what you're talking about," was all I could come up with.

Now Naomi was inspecting the fancy chicken house up close. I had done a great job. Rosie even planted real tiny flowers in the little window boxes. But the cop didn't pay any attention to those. Instead, she was looking at the roof. And that silly weather vane.

"What about this? Did you make this, Rex?"

"No. Rosie added that. It doesn't go at all." I was so annoyed when she put that stupid thing on there. I told her, too.

"Rosie, is it alright if I take it down?" Naomi asked, pretending to be so polite.

"It's all yours." Rosie smiled like they were at a tea party or something. I felt like the mad hatter, with a gun pointed to where my top hat should be.

Naomi carefully pulled the tiny weather vane and the fancy cupola it was attached to off the roof. She turned it upside down and pulled something out of it.

"What is that?" It looked like some kind of battery attached to something electronic.

"Isn't it adorable?" Rosie exclaimed, still using that tea party voice. "It's a camera. Microphone too. All I really wanted to know was what you were doing to scare my poor girls. But it turns out I learned a whole lot more."

I roared and lunged for her. But the cuffs. And the click of the gun aimed at my head. I lost my balance and ended up face down in the filth where the chickens scratched and shit. I rolled to my side, feeling every bruise from the night before, and gave up.

Pops was wrong. Chickens weren't the worst. Women were.

THE CASE OF THE NAKED SCARECROW

Karen A. Phillips

"Russell's naked again."

My five-year-old brother, Billy, stood outside the chicken run as I fed the flock, his chubby fingers clutching the wire fencing while the birds pecked at my feet.

I shielded my eyes against the early morning sun and scanned the cornfield. Sure enough, our scarecrow was indeed missing his clothes.

I frowned. "That's the second time in as many weeks."

"Who wants his clothes?" Billy asked.

I wiped sweat from my brow and sighed. "Beats me, buddy."

It was my last summer on the farm before leaving for college, and I didn't need any complications. I was feeling torn. My parents needed my help, but they insisted I pursue my dream of a degree in graphic design at California State University, Sacramento. I would miss them, but I wouldn't miss the choking dust from the tractors working the fields or the constant caw of crows. I was eager to start a new life in the capital city, one hour and fifteen minutes to the north—close enough for the occasional visit but far enough away to gain my independence. Yet, as exciting as it was, the idea of being alone and vulnerable in a city where I knew no one was a little scary.

***

The roar of a tractor announced the arrival of our father as he rounded the barn and parked. He got up with the sun and usually ate his breakfast while working the fields. Dad took a drink of water from a canteen, opened the cab door and climbed out.

Billy ran over and pointed to Russell while he tugged on Dad's arm. "Look, look."

Dad allowed himself to be led to the edge of the cornfield where they stopped. He pushed his red sweat-stained ball cap back and scratched his forehead. "I'll be damned."

"Whatcha gonna do, Dad?"

"Dunno, son. It's a puzzle."

Mom came out of the house with a bucket of scraps for the pigs. She stopped and the four of us considered the scarecrow, exposed to the elements. He was made of old pillowcases stuffed with straw and attached to a wooden cross. Using a black felt-tip marker, I had made two large triangles for his eyes and a smaller triangle for the nose. I let Billy draw the mouth, which is why Russell smiled at us with crooked lips.

Mom sighed. "Not again. I'm afraid I've run out of your father's old clothes."

Billy looked up at Mom. "I'd give him some of mine, but I'm too small."

"It's a mystery," I said. "If I were Nancy Drew, I'd take the case. Want me to ask Mrs. Harmon if she saw anything?"

The closest neighbor lived down the road, on the other side of the cornfield. They were repaving their driveway. Orange cones had been placed to keep people off the cement while it cured. A white Hyundai was parked on the side of the road.

"It's okay, honey," Mom said. "I've been meaning to have a talk with Mrs. Harmon, and it looks like she's home. I'll ask if she has any used clothing she's willing to part with."

"Penny, why don't you take Billy and look for clues," Dad said to me. "Maybe this time you'll get lucky."

I was tempted to say I'd have more luck if I posted a picture of Russell on Instagram and asked people to help me solve the case. But I'd been taught to obey my elders, so I kept my thoughts to myself and did as instructed.

***

After an hour of fruitless searching, Billy was tired and thirsty. I carried him into the house and settled him on the sofa. I gave him a juice pouch and turned on the TV to his favorite channel.

In my bedroom I grabbed my phone and went back outside, intending to take a photo of Russell, when a black and white Brentwood police car drove down the road. I sprinted after it, waving my arms. The car stopped, and the passenger window slid down. I felt a rush of cold air from the A/C. An attractive man with close-cut black hair and dark sunglasses leaned over the passenger seat.

"What seems to be the trouble, Miss?"

"Officer, I want to report a crime."

The man frowned. "Let me park, and I'll be right with you."

He pulled the car onto our driveway but stayed inside for a few minutes while he talked on the phone.

Finally, the car's engine died and the man stepped out. "Your name, miss?"

"Penny Brite. My family owns Brite Sweetcorn. Are you the officer who patrols this area?"

"I'm Officer Petty," he said with a touch of impatience. "What can I help you with, Miss Brite?"

He followed me to the cornfield where two crows perched on Russell's shoulders.

"Shoo!" I yelled.

The birds flew to the barn roof and observed us with beady eyes.

"Someone stole the clothes off our scarecrow," I said, indicating Russell with my chin. "This is the second time it's happened."

A muscle in Officer Petty's jaw twitched, and I thought he might smile, but his expression remained grim.

"No doubt some local kids pulling a prank. They get bored and look for trouble. I'm sure you know how it is."

I shook my head. "I hardly ever have free time. There's too much to do."

"Once school starts, things will calm down." He pulled a notepad from a pocket. "Describe the clothes and when you noticed them missing."

"They're my dad's old clothes—flannel shirt, jeans." I studied Petty's lanky frame. "He's about your size. Anyway, the clothes were missing this morning. It happened last week, too. Can't remember the exact day, but it's never happened before."

"I'll follow up on it, but, like I said, it's probably nothing." He closed the pad.

Anger flared, and my cheeks grew hot. I squared my shoulders and stood tall. "With all due respect, sir, theft is a crime. Not to mention, the culprit entered our property illegally."

"As I said, Miss, I'll look into it." Petty checked his watch. "I've got another call to make, and I'm running late."

He left our property and parked down the road behind Mrs. Harmon's car. I knew Mr. Harmon worked for one of the state departments in Sacramento. With the commute, he was gone most of the day and often traveled out of town for business. I hoped Mrs. Harmon was okay. Would a person who stooped low enough to steal a scarecrow's clothes be tempted to commit a more serious offense, like taking advantage of a woman home alone?

***

That night, I lay awake worrying. Just because I didn't find any clues didn't mean the crook wasn't lying in wait for one of us to be his next victim. My bedroom window was open to the cool evening breeze. I heard the rhythmic hoot of a great horned owl and another answering back. Then I heard a strange scratch and thump. Was it the criminal? Or a bunch of juvenile delinquents looking for trouble on a summer night? I went to the window and strained to listen, focusing on the slightest sound, but all was quiet except for the gentle rattle of corn stalks in the wind. I shut the window, locked it and closed the blinds. Eventually, I drifted off to sleep.

***

Frustrated by Officer Petty's lack of concern, I decided it was up to me to solve the case of the scarecrow's missing clothes. Brite Sweetcorn sold to local restaurants and grocery stores. Our forty-acre farm was tiny compared to Big Ag—but, nevertheless, the quest was daunting. My parents instilled in me a strong work ethic, and I was determined to leave no stone unturned. I couldn't leave for college with a felon on the loose.

Puffy white clouds hung in the blue sky. I shaded my eyes and looked out over the cornfields, which seemed to stretch forever behind our house and barn. A berm ran along an irrigation ditch. I walked along the elevated ground, searching for a clue. Eventually, I reached the packing shed, which occupied the far corner of our property, bordering the road. The packing shed might seem a good place for a ne'er-do-well to hide, but with the harvest season in full swing, the shed was bustling with activity. I asked a few of the workers if they'd seen anything suspicious, but all shook their heads, no.

I headed back to the house, using a different route, my eyes peeled for any evidence.

My last stop was the old barn, a two-story wooden building with fading red paint. The door creaked when I opened it. Sunbeams filtered through the cracks, but most of the interior was cast in shadow. I stepped inside and the pungent odor of bat guano hit me. All was silent as a tomb except for the faint scurrying of rodents. A ladder reached the hayloft above. Was the bad guy hiding up there? My heart raced and my armpits grew damp. What would Nancy do? I grabbed a hay hook, took a deep breath and climbed, but to my disappointment (and relief) the only thing I found was an owl pellet. Billy would be thrilled.

***

Mom was shucking corn in the kitchen when I came in.

"Did Mrs. Harmon see anything?" I asked. "Did she give you any clothes for Russell?"

"Nope." She stayed focused on the task at hand, ripping the husks from a cob. She grabbed another and repeated the process.

My mother was normally chatty, but for some reason she wasn't in the mood to talk. Again, I wondered if something was going on with Mrs. Harmon. Or perhaps Mom was contemplating my upcoming departure?

"I hope you're not worried about me being away," I said to her. "I'll be fine. And I'll come home often."

The only sound was the tearing of corn husks and the swish of silk falling to the floor.

"If it's about who took Russell's clothes, I'm on it," I said.

"I know, honey. It's not you I'm worried about."

I pulled up a chair and helped shuck while pondering her comment.

***

Russell was still without clothes the next morning. I imagined his shame and averted my gaze.

As I carried a basket of eggs to the house, movement caught my eye. A black and white drove near the Harmon's and parked on the side of the road. A policeman got out and strode to the house.

Mom stopped on her way to feed the pigs. "Something wrong?" she asked.

I frowned. "Is Mrs. Harmon okay? This is the second time I've seen a cop at her house."

"Honey, it's best to mind your own business. How many eggs did you get?"

"I'm pretty sure it's Officer Petty. I told him about the theft of Russell's clothes and how someone had trespassed onto our farm, but he dismissed me. Said it was probably just some local kids."

Mom gazed at the Harmon home. "Officer Petty needs to learn a lesson."

I stared at Mom, unsure of her meaning.

***

I was rummaging through my closet when Mom came into my bedroom.

"Whatcha doing?"

"Looking for clothes to dress Russell. I feel sorry for him." I held up a pink floral print blouse with ruffled sleeves. "How 'bout this?"

"Your grandmother gave you that for your birthday last year."

"I know, Mom, but it's not really my style."

She sighed.

"Grandma won't know," I said. "Besides, she only visits once a year."

I found a pair of ratty sweatpants and a yellow floppy sun hat.

Mom grinned. "I dare say Russell will scare more than crows in that outfit."

***

KABOOM!

I ran out of the house as crows took to the sky, cawing their displeasure. Down the road, Mr. Harmon stood in front of his house, brandishing a shotgun. Mrs. Harmon was on her knees, clutching a bed sheet to her bare chest, pleading with her husband for mercy.

At that moment, Officer Petty sprinted by, dressed only in a familiar pink blouse with ruffled sleeves. I admired his firm buttocks as he disappeared into the cornfields.

***

The next morning, I went outside to begin my chores and found a shopping bag on the porch. A note taped to the bag read, TO RUSSELL, FROM MR. HARMON.

I noticed Officer Petty's car was no longer parked on the side of the road. When did he retrieve his patrol car? He must've hid out for hours until the coast was clear.

Mr. Harmon's car was nowhere to be seen, and I assumed he'd gone to work after dropping the bag at our house. I wondered if he intended to file a complaint about Officer Petty. Or maybe not, feeling confident he'd made his point with the help of a double-barrel.

Just before lunchtime, Mom received a phone call from another neighbor, Mrs. Peabody. The Peabody boys had been caught getting into mischief. She put them on the phone, and they apologized to Mom for stealing Russell's clothes. They volunteered to work on the farm in exchange for our forgiveness.

Through the kitchen window, I saw a black and white driving slowly down the road.

I ran outside.

Was it Officer Petty? I couldn't believe he'd dare to return. Then I remembered the boy I had a crush on in high school and the stupid things I did to get his attention. I deduced Officer Petty must be powerfully attracted to Mrs. Harmon.

As the patrol car passed our house, it suddenly lurched to a stop and the passenger-side window rolled down. Officer Petty removed his sunglasses and gaped at our scarecrow. Then he jammed the car in reverse, made a U-turn and sped off, laying rubber on the pavement.

I turned around and gave Russell a big smile. I had to admit, he cut a fine figure dressed in his Brentwood PD uniform.

DEAR JOHN DEERE

Chris Dreith

The case became more interesting as soon as we found the crumpled letter in the middle of the dirty barn floor.

The deputies could have found it easily, but they made zero effort. They just glanced into the old wooden structure on the Deere Family Farm to make sure the new tractor was missing, made their report, and left.

That's when Jane Deere called us for help. My name is Melvin Dun. Mel, to my friends, and I am very particular about who I call a friend. My partner, Wendy Gita and I run the Sacramento firm, Gita Dun Investigations, specializing in whatever might bring in some dough.

Jane and her brother, John's, place is on the Yolo County side of the Sacramento River where they grow Real Organic tomatoes. Don't ask Jane what the difference is between Real Organic and just plain Organic. You will be stuck for hours, listening to her harp on the increasing politics in product labeling and the dwindling profits in agriculture.

According to Jane, the John Deere Series 9RX830 Tractor, no relation she insists, was parked in the barn yesterday, and now it's gone.

"Oh, by the way, John is missing, too," she added as she stepped into her 2024 Ram 2500 Power Wagon pickup and tore new ruts through the farmyard to the River Road.

"She coulda led with that," Wendy said once the dust settled.

"All I heard was the reward she offered for the tractor's return," I spit the fine particles of dirt from my mouth. "We could make a few back rent payments with that."

Wendy pulled up the specs of the 9RX 830 on her phone as we walked toward the barn.

"Holy cow! That's one big-A tractor!" she flipped her screen toward me so I could see what we were looking for. "I never knew there was that much money in tomatoes," she shook her head. "Over a million dollars for a tractor?"

"Naw," I said. "Probably not all from tomatoes. I've known the family for years. Jane and John inherited the place and could barely make a go of it until John won big in the lottery back in 2022."

"Oh yeah," I had Wendy's attention now. "I remember some farmer won several million dollars. And they are still farming?"

"John is. He loves it. But Jane is now a 'financial advisor' and has moved into a big fancy house in Granite Bay, Folsom, or somewhere like that."

We walked past the rusty camper that had been disintegrating into the land for as long as I could remember. The flimsy curtains hanging crooked in the window made me cringe. I really didn't want to look inside. Who knew what might be in there?

"Let's start with the barn," I suggested.

We stood outside the large opening and looked into the gaping space.

"The deputies were right," Wendy announced unnecessarily. "The 9RX 830 isn't here."

It was easy to see the wide four-track prints in the dust and follow them out of the barn where we lost them in the yard. Our car, the deputies, and Jane's monster truck had wiped out any evidence that could give us a clue as to which way the tractor might have gone.

Back in the barn, Wendy snapped on Nitrile gloves and handed a set to me. She grabbed my shoulder for balance as she pulled the paper booties over her shoes and made sure I didn't fall when I did the same. We are both retired from law enforcement, and this process was ingrained in us. She had more than thirty-four years with Sacramento County Sheriff's Office, and I had a little more with Yolo County. We were both a bit long in the tooth, but not dead yet.

"I'll do the left perimeter; you start on the right," I said, but probably didn't need to. She was already combing the right side of the building.

After more than an hour of searching for clues through straw, wooden crates, and old rusty metal things that I had no idea the purpose of, we met in the middle. The only thing I had put in the transparent plastic evidence bag was a partial rat carcass, thinking it would be fun to freak Wendy out when she saw it. However, she had the same thing in her evidence bag, so we dumped both rat bodies and proceeded to move down the center of the barn together.

I took several shots of the tractor's unique tread on the surface of the dirt floor with my phone and was enlarging them to make sure they were clear when Wendy bent over and said, "Hmmm."

She lifted a crumpled pink paper by the corner with the pair of tweezers she always brings along and gently pulled the note open with her gloved thumb and index finger. We both leaned forward and read:

Dear John Deere,

It's been sweet, but our time together will never come to fruition. Unfortunately, you were not able to produce the quality I needed to reap from this relationship.

Sincerely,
Cherry Tomahdo
Personal Chef, Social Media Influencer, and Event Planner
Tomato Tomahdo Events
Cherry@TomatoTomahdoEvents.com
916-666-6660 666 County Rd. 13, Rio Linda, CA 95666

"Hmmm," Wendy said, again. "A bit harsh."

"Well, it is a Dear John letter," I said. "Supposed to be harsh."

"Ever heard of Cherry Tomahdo?"

"Nope, can't say as I have," I was thinking the name sounded more like a stripper or pole dancer, but I have learned not to make such sexist remarks out loud around Wendy.

"Sounds like a stripper or pole dancer," Wendy muttered.

I choked back a laugh.

We carefully put the Dear John letter in another plastic evidence bag and walked out of the barn toward the only other structure in the farmyard.

At the camper door, I hesitated. Wendy patted me on the back and took the lead. She knew I hated going into places like that. I've had a few bad experiences in creepy, tight spaces.

The screen hung uselessly to the side as Wendy pushed the aluminum door open. It squealed on its hinges, and I almost did, too. A waft of musky odor escaped with a cloud of flies.

"Uh oh," I shut my eyes.

"Don't be a baby," Wendy said. I heard her paper booties swish across the floor. I was taking deep breaths, my hand covering my mouth, hoping I wouldn't gag, when she said, "It's not what you think."

I opened my eyes and saw a mess on the little kitchen counter; a large knife lay on the floor.

"It's tomatoes," Wendy said before I could bolt.

"What?"

"Tomatoes," she said. "Someone cut up a bunch of tomatoes and left them all over the counter. What a mess. Flies everywhere."

I took a cautious step through the door and looked around. Besides the dribbly red mess, the place was cleaner than I had expected. Cushions with faded plaid fabric covered two small bench seats facing a wood-look Formica table. I could see a bed with the same plaid fabric through a short hallway at the other end of the camper. Wendy walked in that direction, which gave me a good excuse not to move far from the door.

"Nothing in here," she called from the tiny bedroom. I was starting to feel my heart rate slow down.

"Looks like John might be living here," she said, walking back to the kitchenette. She stopped in front of the only framed picture on the wall and pointed to the smiling face of John Deere holding a giant check made out to him from the California Lottery for thirty-seven million dollars. I snapped a photo of it in case we needed it to identify John. Why we would need to ID him was a thought I tried to push out of my mind.

"Imagine winning millions and ending up living in a place like this," Wendy ran her finger around the edge of the counter.

"There's a bunch of papers on the table. Maybe he was just using this place as a farm office," I suggested.

We both rifled through the paperwork. Most had to deal with information from the local tomato canneries and water district reports, but a few were posters advertising the upcoming Tower Bridge Dinner.

Wendy picked up a poster. "Ever attend this? It's happening tonight."

"Are you kidding? Tickets are like $300 each. Besides, I don't think I would fit in," I said.

"Hmmm," Wendy said, still reading the poster. I wondered if she wanted to belong to that crowd.

"Do you think John Deere would?" she asked. "I mean, he's rich. And he's a farmer. An organic one at that. The Bridge Dinner is all about Farm To Fork, right?" She held up the poster for me to see.

"Yeah. But the John Deere I know probably wouldn't feel comfortable. His sister Jane, now, that's her deal. I can see her there, schmoozing and networking." I could easily imagine Jane Deere at the long, elegant tables that covered the bridge over the Sacramento River for the annual event.

"Well, it looks like he was interested in the chefs," Wendy pointed at the circled names of the celebrity chefs who were expected to create something fabulous for the dinner. One name was underlined several times.

"Chef Giovanni Fieri," she said. "Mmm, nice!"

I tried not to imagine what she meant by that comment.

"So," Wendy started. "Are we assuming John took the tractor? If so, it's his tractor, right? No theft. No reward. But what if someone else stole it and kidnapped John while they were at it?"

"Follow the evidence, kid," I warned. "We just need more information.

Wendy nodded and we spent a few silent moments to let our own thoughts settle.

"I think we're done here," I suggested. "How about we try to find Ms. Tomahdo and see if she knows where John is? That letter made it sound like they had some sort of relationship. If we can find John, we can probably find the tractor."

Wendy continued to look at the poster, finally folded it up, stuck it in her pocket, and said, "Sure. That's a good idea."

***

No one came to Cherry Tomahdo's apartment door when we knocked except a frantic, yappy Chihuahua. Through the balcony window, we watched the dog bounce up and down until a neighbor's door opened.

"Cherry's not home," the neighbor said over the irritating noise. "And that dog is going to continue to bark and bounce until it passes out if you stand there long enough."

She motioned us away from the window and into her apartment. Wendy shrugged and followed her inside. I took another look at the frenzied little dog, decided to give it a break, and stepped into the neighbor's place, too.

The apartment was an extravagant mass of flowery prints. Wallpaper, carpet, upholstery, and window coverings all had different floral impressions. Even the neighbor had on a flowing dress with rose prints, a fake flower lei, and a bundle of plastic daisies in her hair. It was staggering and disorienting to me, but she stood solidly in the middle of the clutter and smiled.

"See?" she said. "Bernardo stopped barking. I swear that little thing is going to explode someday."

She motioned us to sit. Wendy took the tulip chair, I sat down on the California Poppy couch.

"Now, what can I help you with?" Tomahdo's neighbor asked as she plopped into a red Lazy Boy recliner with lavender print pillows.

"We are looking for Ms. Tomahdo," Wendy stated. She didn't seem to be affected by the visual dizziness.

"Actually, we are searching for this man," I brought up John's picture with the Lottery check and showed the screen to the neighbor. She leaned forward to get a good look.

"Ah, yes," she said. "I might have seen him. It's hard to be precise, you know. Cherry is quite popular. She has many gentlemen callers."

The neighbor sat back in her chair and fluttered her hands.

"Oh, my! Where are my manners," she giggled. "I haven't even introduced myself yet. I'm Daisy Fields and I am Cherry Tomahdo's bestie."

Wendy introduced us both. "We've been hired to find a missing farm implement," she explained. "And we think Ms. Tomahdo might know where the owner is." She pointed to the photo that was still on my screen.

"Oh, dear," Daisy Fields said, a frown started growing on her face. "I'm sure Cherry didn't take a farm implement."

"Oh, no," Wendy hurriedly assured her. "I'm sure she didn't either. We are just trying to get information about where John might be."

A smile, a nod from Wendy, and Ms. Fields relaxed.

"Well, Cherry has been very busy lately," she said. "She is involved with all sorts of wonderful events, you know. She is an actual personal chef and a social media influencer, besides being an event planner." She nodded her head and waited for us to be impressed.

"That sounds exciting," Wendy said. She could always move a conversation along better than I could, so I kept my mouth shut.

"It is," exclaimed Ms. Fields. "Do you know about that Bridge dinner?" She didn't give us any time to respond, which was fine with me. "Cherry has had most of the chefs to her apartment." Her voice went down to a whisper. "Especially that Italian chef.... what's his name?" Her fingers were fluttering again.

"Chef Giovanni Fieri?" Wendy managed to keep her excitement contained.

"That's the one." Ms. Fields clapped her hands.

"Well, that helps us tremendously," Wendy quickly stood up. "Thank you so much, Ms. Fields."

"Daisy," she said. "Please just call me Daisy. And stop by anytime."

Ms. Fields seemed surprised that we were leaving so soon. Frankly, I was, too, but managed to push myself up from the couch in time to make it out the door with Wendy. We hurried down the sidewalk as Bernardo started ramping up for another barking frenzy.

"What's your hurry?" I asked as Wendy yanked open the car door.

"The Tower Bridge Dinner is tonight," she said, shoving the key in the ignition. "We should find Giovanni."

"Oooookay," I was trying to make sense of her rush and just got my door closed and safety belt almost latched when she took off.

"It's simple, Mel," she said. "If Tomahdo has something to do with the Bridge Dinner and Chef Giovanni Fieri, she would probably be working on it now since the event is scheduled to happen in just a few hours."

"So, we are off to the Tower Bridge?"

"No," Wendy said as she cut around a driver on our right who was apparently moving too slow for her. "We should stop by the Delta King first. That's where the celebrity chefs have been staying."

"Hold on," I said. Thoughts were starting to run off the rails. "We were hired to find the tractor. And John. Not this Giovanni guy."

She shrugged, smiled, and hit the gas.

***

Henry Madsen stood on the dock in front of the historic paddlewheel riverboat, the Delta King, which had been moored along the Old Sacramento Waterfront since 1927. The Delta King had been beautifully restored and converted to a boutique hotel with an excellent restaurant and bar.

Henry was an old friend from my Sheriff Department days and was now the head of security for the King. His muscled arms were crossed over his broad chest, his feet planted wide apart and he looked angrier than I had ever seen him.

A 'Closed' sign swung from the chain railing of the gangplank next to him.

"What's up, Henry?" I asked as Wendy and I walked toward the big boat.

"Damn TBD crowd," he growled and nodded downriver toward the Tower Bridge.

We could easily see the activity on the bridge from this short distance. The Dinner was being set up. The roadway across the bridge had been closed to make way for the event. White tablecloths were waving gently in the breeze, the reflection of thousands of tiny lights rippled across the surface of the river. Service people scurried back and forth from the massive trucks parked at the foot of the bridge on both sides of the river.

"I would have thought it would be a big night for the King," Wendy said exactly what I was thinking. "The Bridge Dinner is always sold out, but many people would like to come here to watch the action."

"It woulda been a big night for us," Henry snarled, "if it wasn't for a certain chef who tried to destroy our kitchen."

We were interrupted by a happy, well-dressed group advancing toward the gate. Their enthusiasm was immediately doused as Henry explained that Delta King's kitchen was currently closed due to excessive damage. Despite the handful of gift cards he distributed, the hungry crowd left upset.

"That 'certain chef' wouldn't have been that Italian guy, would it?" I asked Henry when he returned to us.

He rolled his eyes. "Italian, bull," he said. "The guy's a fake. I heard he was from Fresno."

"No," Wendy seemed to deflate.

Henry nodded. "Yup. A couple of the other chefs said he came up with an Italian accent just to get on the Food Channel, but they knew him from when he bussed tables at the Spaghetti Factory in Fresno."

"What happened in the kitchen?" I tried not to gloat. Wendy was feeling bad and she was my partner. I should support her, but man, it was funny.

"Apparently, the fake Italian chef said he was getting some special tomatoes for his dish from his supplier," Henry said. "Turns out, one of the other chefs discovered the tomatoes came from a hot-house in Mexico."

He rolled his eyes. "This event is supposed to highlight local food, and all that, but when the 'Italian' was outed, he tried to convince the other chefs there wasn't a difference. Chopped up his tomatoes and some of the local ones and demanded the other chefs taste them to see if they could tell any difference. Turns out, they all could.

"He went ballistic. Started throwing tomatoes around and advanced to throwing all the choppers, cleavers, and knives he could grab. Kitchen help was screaming and running every which way. By the time we wrestled him to the ground, he'd been able to sever the plumbing lines, but the vent hood cables were cut and he was working on dismantling the grill."

"Good grief," Wendy said. "Is he OK?"

Both Henry and I took a moment.

"Ah, Wendy," Henry said through gritted teeth. "I was more worried about the kitchen help and the customers than that jerk fake chef."

"I think what Wendy meant to ask," I placed a heavy hand on her shoulder, which was our code for Do Not Talk, "was, is he in jail? We think he might know something about the case we are on. We'd like to talk to him."

"Nope," Henry scowled. "The folks from Visit Sacramento got involved and paid off the Delta King to not press charges so the Bridge Dinner wouldn't have bad press."

He continued to mutter curses under his breath.

"You know where we might find him?" I asked.

Henry indicated toward the bridge. "Probably up on the bridge. The media is showing up, so he's probably in front of a camera by now." He shook his head again and walked toward another group of advancing diners looking forward to their fancy meal on the King, soon to be disappointed.

I kept my hand on Wendy's shoulder, directing her south along the wooden boardwalk. When we arrived at the Tower Bridge, news vans crowned with satellite dishes were jousting for space at the river's edge. The crews were hoisting heavy cameras on their shoulders and checking the light and sound equipment.

A tall man dressed in a crisp white chef's coat that matched his brilliantly white toothy smile stood near them. A stressed woman was fussing with his hair, making sure every strand was perfectly combed straight back from his handsome face.

I heard Wendy take a quick inhale. This must be the fake Italian we were looking for.

"He looks like Gavin Newsom," I said.

She tilted her head. "Don't see it," she responded.

We pushed our way through to stand in front of him. He turned, offering us the full force of his beam. I noticed some bronzer had rubbed from his cheek onto the shoulder of his coat, but Wendy didn't seem to see it. I decided not to point it out.

"Alo!" he said. "Wheech station are you weeth?" Was he really kissing Wendy's hand? Good grief.

"We aren't with the press," I said.

He immediately dropped her hand and stood back, his smile a bit more forced. "Ah," was all he said as his eyes scanned the media crowd.

"We're trying to locate Cherry Tomahdo," Wendy said.

The fake chef's face turned to stone. His cold eyes met ours briefly when he said, without a trace of Italian accent, "Don't know where that bitc...." He stopped talking and tried to regain his desired persona.

"Scusa me. I do na know such a person," his eyes sweeping the news vans again.

"Can it, Fresno," Wendy said. "We know all about you and Tomahdo."

The chef froze. The harried woman was reaching to adjust one loose thread of hair, but he pushed her away. He leaned toward us and whispered, "What do you want?"

"Where's Tomahdo?" Wendy asked again.

"I don't know. She's been trying to ruin me." He glanced again at the reporters who looked ready to interview him. It was comical to see him try to change the angry expression on his face to something he wished to be on camera. A quick wave to the media, and he bent toward us, conspiratorially.

"Look," he said in a whisper. "What can I offer you to keep your mouths shut?"

"What happened with Tomahdo?" Wendy whispered back. "Tell us now, and we'll get out of your hair." She took a quick look at his glossy hair gel, and I almost laughed out loud.

"I hired her to increase my media presence and to find me the best tomatoes around. My dish for this dinner is bruschetta. All she brought me were different colored, random-sized, old tomatoes. I can't use that! I told her those weren't up to my high standards."

"Old tomatoes?" Wendy asked. "You mean, like Heritage Tomatoes?"

"Yeah, that's it," he said.

Wendy and I looked at each other. What kind of a chef is this guy?

She turned back to him. "So, you decided to get hot-house tomatoes from Mexico instead?"

"You heard about that?" He was squirming now.

We both nodded.

"I called her late last night after the Delta King incident," he sighed. "I told her to get me those old tomatoes or I wasn't going to pay her, but she's not here yet. I'm going to have to tell the press I couldn't find the quality I was looking for."

Was that a tear in his eye?

"I'm going to sue her ass," he growled.

"Giovanni! Chef Fieri!" A beautiful young woman with long, black hair flowing over one shoulder of her Channel 13 News jacket was pushing toward us with her microphone pointing at the fake Signor Giovanni. We stepped back as other news reporters and paparazzi gathered around him. His sham-chef guise reappeared as he welcomed his fans. He was definitely in his element.

Wendy leaned toward me and said quietly, "Newsom. Yeah. I see it now."

I was proud of her.

Suddenly, a loud crunching sound echoed across the bridge from the Yolo County side. High screams followed, and people were frantically running toward us. A deep rumble, the heavy metal bridge seemed to vibrate, and the front of a gigantic green tractor appeared on the bridge with a shovel loader full of red, orange, and green plants raised high in the air. The monster slowly crawled forward, smashing tables and chairs under its four wide tracks. Bits and pieces of the rented furniture were sent flying over the rails of the bridge and into the water. It was like watching a 1950s Godzilla movie, except in color. I couldn't stop staring.

Thankfully, the behemoth came to a panting stop in the middle of the bridge before it hit us. I could feel the media crowd's excitement when a pink-haired woman popped out of the tractor's cab with a microphone in her hand.

"Ya want the best tomatoes around; ya fake?" her voice boomed. Then she ducked back into the glassed cab, pounded on a large computer screen, looked up with a giant grin when the bucket of the shovel loader started tilting forward. It screeched a bit as it dumped its load of tomatoes and dirt onto the middle of the bridge, splattering across the remaining tables and the watching crowd.

For a brief moment, everything was quiet. Then the media went crazy.

"Well, I guess we found the tractor," Wendy said.

I nodded but wasn't sure we would be able to collect the reward.

Behind the 9RX830, a slim figure stumbled into view at the edge of the bridge and grabbed the railing near the pedestrian walkway. John Deere looked exhausted. I ran to him and wrapped my arms around his shaking form before he collapsed.

"John! What the heck?" I said as I checked him over for obvious wounds.

"Hey, Mel," he squeaked. "That woman is crazy."

Wendy found a chair that hadn't been smashed, and we were able to gently lower John onto it. He leaned back, trying to catch his breath.

"I've been chasing her for hours," he wheezed.

"On foot?" Wendy asked.

John nodded. "I saw her sneaking around the barn at about dawn." He took a breath. "She had arranged to purchase a container of Heritage tomatoes from me several weeks ago for some famous chef."

He watched as the security crew tried to remove Ms. Tomahdo from the tractor's air-conditioned cab.

"Then she sent me a Dear John letter, telling me my tomatoes weren't good enough." His face reddened as he told us about it, obviously in shock that anyone would ever consider his produce sub-par.

"I was in the old camper this morning checking the tomatoes to see if there really was a problem with the quality. There wasn't," he said defiantly. "I heard the tractor start in the barn and knew someone was stealing it. When I ran outside, I saw her fiddling with the on-board computers. They aren't the easiest thing to use."

We nodded.

"But she figured it out before I could climb up into the cab and she drove the dang thing right out of the barn. I ran after her but couldn't catch up. She got on the River Road and then plowed right into one of my tomato fields. Ruined several rows. They was just about ready for harvest."

"Sorry, man," I patted his shoulder.

"That crazy woman just scooped a bunch of whole plants and soil up and started this way. I think she didn't know how to get to the bridge through West Sacramento cuz it took us all day. We ran through several neighborhoods. Can't believe no one called the cops. People just stood in their front yards and watched us go by. My tractor isn't meant to drive through residential neighborhoods, and I'm certainly not meant to run that far!"

His head dropped toward his chest and I heard a few sobs. "I just couldn't catch up enough to climb in the cab and stop her," his voice was cracking, but he mustered up enough strength when the police came over, to be able to tell the whole story.

***

Needless to say, the Tower Bridge Dinner had to be rescheduled, but the media had a wonderful night. Not only did they get great footage of the tomato dump, but they were also able to break the 'fake news' story regarding Chef Giovanni Fieri, whose real name was Ferlin Wells.

Jane Deere was hesitant to pay us the reward but eventually did when John insisted. After being interviewed on camera at the site of the Big Tomato Dump, as the media named it, John became a local favorite and has become the farming expert for Channel 13. Jane determined that could generate higher profits for the next harvest season, so all is good.

Wendy and I celebrated with a dinner on the Delta King after Henry let us know when the kitchen repairs were completed.

No tomatoes were on the menu.

FARM TO FINGERS

Virginia V. Kidd

Another cookbook. Lexi added it to the stack on the table. The Friends of McClatchy Library gratefully accepted whatever used books came in as donations. But really, she thought, enough with the cookbooks! The Friends would never sell all these to the people of Sacramento.

"Are you pulling out the boring books that don't have stories in them?" The shrill voice startled her. Shannon, of course. It was always Shannon. Lexi sighed. The eight-year-old was not supposed to be in the Friends of the Library workroom, but here she was. The girl came dangerously close to knocking the book stack over as she pulled herself up, resting her midriff on the table edge to ask Lexi, "Do police make people in prison read books that don't have stories?"

"Get down please, Shannon." Today the girl wore red canvas shoes, blue jean shorts, and a pale green tee shirt featuring Harvey Girls. It was from the Sacramento Train Museum, Lexi knew. The child's small fingers sported turquoise nails colored by what looked to Lexi like the work of a Sharpie.

"We're planning our summer book sale," Lexi said as the girl dropped down to her feet. "Many people like books about food even without stories." Or they did before they could get recipes for free on the internet. However, she admitted to herself, the reading community no longer clamored for recipes to make elaborate but time-consuming dishes. "These books tell them how to cook the fresh food that grows around here. Sacramento is the Farm-to-Fork capital, you know."

"Yes, I know, and it's wrong. It should be Farm-to-Fingers." Now perched on a tape-closed box labeled BIOGRAPHIES, Shannon pulled raisins out of her jeans pocket and smacked them into her mouth, a handful at a time. "Who eats raisins with a fork?" she queried as she chewed. "Or almonds? Or carrot sticks? Or pears from the Pear Fair? I bet somebody like my Grandma Lois came up with that fork thing. She has all kind of rules about how to eat that she calls 'manners.' Billy and I can't even have watermelon seed spitting contests at her house anymore. Look at this!" Shannon held up a cookbook featuring a lemon and a lemon meringue pie on the cover. "Who eats a lemon with a fork? Farm-to-Fingers, I say."

On the point of telling Shannon that nobody directly ate lemons with or without a fork, Lexi noticed a note sticking out of the next donated book. Later, she would claim she felt icicles rolling up her spine when she pulled the note out. At the time, however, she just saw it as forgotten clutter. On the note she saw: "If you read this, help me," scrawled in smeared blue ink. Was it a cry for help? Then why wasn't it signed? Who would she help? What help was needed? Where? How? It was just a spur-of-the-moment bookmark, she reasoned; it was identifying a favorite recipe—no, a difficult recipe. "Help me" didn't have to be a person in trouble. It could be a plea for kitchen assistance, for someone to chop the celery or zest the lemon or grate the cheese. And the dark swirl at the base of the paper was—ketchup? Soy sauce? Barbecue marinade? Not blood. Surely not human blood.

What book was this? She held it up to see the title: *Sweet and Healthy* with the subtitle *Making Desserts with Vegetables*. She thumbed through the pages: carrot cake, zucchini bread, garden vegetable pie, cauliflower pie crust, turnip cake, Brussels sprout chocolate chip cake. She shuddered. No wonder it was donated!

"That was Claudia's book," Shannon said. "I saw it at her house. She likes vegetables. She grows them in her garden in her back yard, not on a farm. Instead of Farms to Fingers we could be the city of Gardens to Stomachs. Gardens to Guts, that sounds better, doesn't it? Claudia disappeared without saying goodbye, and she left Cosmo locked out of her apartment. He meowed so loud Mama let him come into our place, and he came right up and ate part of my tuna sandwich and sleeps with me now. I hope Claudia doesn't come back. Then he'll be mine forever."

Claudia disappeared? She'd been in the library Thursday, Lexi knew. Was 'disappeared' a child's explanation or ... Lexi shot a quick glance at the note again. Shannon continued on her earlier theme. "Maybe saying *fork* was this author. I've seen her on TV." Her face a frown, she stabbed a finger on a Martha Stewart cookbook featuring a beautifully-set table. "Why would someone spend time decorating a table when they could be solving mysteries with Trixie Beldon or Nancy Drew?"

Thinking that the girl had a point. Lexi replied, "Or Kinsey Millhone or Jane Marple? Get down off the books, please, Shannon. What does Claudia grow in her garden?"

"Tomatoes and peppers and eggs."

"Claudia grows eggs? Really?"

"She does, Lexi. She has a tomato plant and a pepper plant and an eggplant. She showed me her eggplant. She wants me to eat one. Mama said eggs come from chickens. I think that's just as disgusting as a plant that grows them. I'm not eating those things for breakfast. Cinnamon rolls must be better for me. There isn't a cinnamon roll plant, is there?"

"No, they're baked. But Shannon, language is confusing you here. An eggplant is a vegetable itself. It really has nothing to do with eggs. It's sort of like a zucchini or a squash. Do you like zucchini or squash?"

"No." Shannon continued her news update: "Cosmo doesn't like vegetables or forks. He likes his food to move, but when it does, sometimes the big orange cat from the blue house gets the food first. His name is Tangerine, and he's naughty. He eats butterflies. He'd eat my tuna, too, if he got it before Cosmo. Cats believe in Farm to Paws. Maybe Air to Paws."

"Is Cosmo in your house now?"

"Yes. You can't have Cosmo; he's mine now. He won't buy your Friends' books. He can't read. He tries to write in books with his claws. Tangerine bites the corners. Those two cats're bad. Lots of cats are really nice to books. Grandma Beth goes to a bookstore in the town where she lives that has a cat named Midnight. He likes to sleep on big books called dictionaries. Have you heard of them?"

Lexi swallowed. When did dictionaries become rarities? "Yes," she nodded. "Dictionaries tell you what words mean."

"They're in computers now, Daddy said," Shannon told her. "Cosmo likes to sleep on Daddy's laptop. But he can't read the words in it. Mama doesn't know how basic he is, so she speaks to him in English. "'Don't claw the sofa, Cosmo,' she says. He doesn't know what she tells him, and he keeps doing it. If he learned words on the computer, he could understand them. Then he wouldn't be in trouble. Claudia really loves him. I don't see why she would leave him without even asking me to feed him."

Maybe she was forced, Lexi thought. "How long has she been gone?"

"Since Sunday."

Two days. "Does anyone else know you usually take care of Cosmo when Claudia is gone?"

Shannon nodded. "Santa. He left Cosmo's presents at my house when Claudia was gone last Christmas. He left Cosmo a big squashy pillow. I went over and got it this morning, so Cosmo'd feel at home with us and sleep on it on my bed and maybe not be lonely."

"That's very kind, Shannon. Cosmo must love you."

Shannon gave a wide grin. "He sits on me and purrs."

Lexi loaded the cookbooks she had stacked into a cardboard box. "Is your mom here at the library today?"

Shannon's eyes widened. "Yes. Am I in trouble?"

"No. I just hoped she might know where Claudia is."

"She doesn't. She asked me where Claudia'd gone. Cosmo might know, but like I told you, he's no good with English. Or Spanish either. Rosa tried talking to him *en español*. That's what she calls it. Computers ought to help cats talk to their humans."

"That would be good, wouldn't it? When they were going to the vet we could explain that it was to get them well. They would feel better about that."

"They wouldn't believe it. Vets give shots like doctors do. Cats would run away like Claudia."

"Did Claudia run away?"

"Well, she's not here."

"What would she run from?"

"Maybe Jimmy. He's her friend, but he gets mad and yells."

"Does Claudia have a cell phone?"

Shannon nodded. "Of course."

"Do you know her number?"

"Yes. It's a math problem. She's a teacher. They can be sort of crazy about arithmetic even in the summer. All phone numbers start with 916."

"Yes, that's right around here."

"Then 5 and 4 are 9."

"916-549, is that right?"

"Yep. Then 6 and 7 are 13. It's too easy. She said she wished she had 6 times 7 is 42. But she didn't have 4 times 5, so she didn't get 6 times 7. That's the way math is. Very rigid. And also very tiresome. Schools should only teach art and reading."

Tiresome or not, Lexi tried the numbers, drawing unanswered rings and an option for voice mail. "Hi, Claudia, this is Lexi from the Friends of the Library. Thank you for the books you donated. Please call me back when you get this. It's about your cat, Cosmo." That ought to get a response, she hoped. "Maybe she left a note at her house," Lexi told Shannon. "You must have a key to her house. Don't you?"

Shannon nodded firmly, her hair flapping toward her face, then away. "From the azalea pot. Maybe Claudia was kidnapped," Shannon suggested. "She's not a kid. Is it called something else when a grown up is taken?"

"Abducted," Lexi supplied, telling herself to think of it as vocabulary building for Shannon. Had Claudia been abducted? In truth, the only sign that Claudia wasn't just out and about somewhere on her own, say San Francisco on a shopping spree, was that she did not ask Shannon to feed the cat and hadn't returned Lexi's call. Claudia could have already fed Cosmo breakfast before she left, possibly something yummy for carnivores from the Natural Foods Co-op. And maybe she had left dry cat food in a bowl somewhere that Cosmo knew to find. Would he have needed more? Say, a tuna sandwich? Big cats always wanted more, Lexi believed. Claudia was not obligated to tell anyone where she was going. Which made her that much more vulnerable if someone—what had Shannon called Claudia's friend who got mad and yelled? Jimmy. If Jimmy wanted Claudia with him somewhere, he could make her go with him. Where? And why?

En route to Claudia's house, they passed Shannon's mom. Nicole offered no suggestions about where Claudia might be.

"Could someone have forced her to go somewhere?" Lexi asked

"I suppose it's possible the way things are these days," Nicole answered. "But who? That bully, Jimmy? But why?"

"Jimmy is a bully?" Lexi asked Nicole, but Shannon answered.

"Yes, and he's going straight to hell, and when he's there, ravens will pick out his eyes."

Nicole looked shocked. "Where did you get that? Did your daddy say that?"

Shannon nodded. "It's true, isn't it?"

Nicole rubbed her forehead as she nodded. "Your daddy is a tad too concerned with Claudia's problems."

"Jimmy abused her?" Lexi asked.

Nicole sighed. "Well, they had differences. Shannon, stay away from their problems."

"Mama, I have to get some cat food and see if she's home."

In Claudia's apartment, they found no disruption, but water stood in the bathtub.

"It's shallow water," Shannon stepped barefoot into the tub in her shorts. Water covered each foot only to her ankle. "Something must have happened here. Claudia wouldn't turn on water for no reason. That wastes water."

"She must have washed something. Maybe Claudia wanted to clean her feet. She wears sandals a lot, doesn't she? She could have washed her feet and left to take that book to the library."

Shannon defended her friend. "She would have drained the tub first."

"Maybe she wanted to give Cosmo a bath when she got back," Lexi suggested.

"Cats do not like that."

"No, they don't," Lexi agreed.

"Cosmo might get in and drown. He wouldn't know how to push this knob down." Shannon pushed it down to start the tub draining, then charged, "She was abducted by a water waster. Probably one who uses plastic bottles and doesn't recycle."

A true villain, Lexi thought, recognizing to herself that today's kids knew bad guys when they saw them damage the environment. "But where is she now?" she wondered.

"Lexi?" Shannon rocked her body back and forth.

Lexi thought she was shy about what she was going to say.

"Do you think—with Claudia gone—should I pick her tomatoes? They're red and look so juicy. I bet they're really good."

"Yes, why not? Are they cherry tomatoes—little ones? Let me take a picture of her plant first. Claudia will want to see it full of tomatoes. Save her some to taste. Do you need a bag or a bowl to put them in?"

Shannon chose a paper bag. She bounded downstairs, wet feet and all.

Pulling out a folded paper bag from a kitchen drawer, Lexi ordered herself to be an adult; but nonetheless she asked, "Any eggs on the eggplant?"

"Let's go see." Shannon started out.

Where was Claudia? Outside, Lexi looked around, hoping for a sight of Claudia's car. She saw an orange fruit rolling through the dark green grass and concluded that Tangerine was aptly named. Cosmo, in contrast, could be a fluff of loose gray fur blown behind him by an erratic wind. Watching Shannon grab up the gray cat, Lexi heard Cosmo let out a loud, rumbling purr.

Lexi snapped photos of Claudia's produce with her cell phone, then asked, "Shannon, where is Claudia's car? Does she have a garage?"

Shannon, further illustrating Farm to Fingers, had stuffed her mouth with fresh cherry tomatoes. She shrugged.

"Does she have a garage?"

The answer, uttered through a full mouth, seemed to be "In the alley."

Alleys in Sacramento have names that start with the letter of the alphabet street that precedes the alley. Thus Tomato Alley came after T Street and before U Street. Following what she could decipher of Shannon's instructions, as well as following the girl herself, Lexi started down Tomato Alley, a fairly unused cracked concrete roadway lined with garage doors below two-story apartments. Dark blue dumpsters sat across the alley from long wooden fences that protected back yards of houses facing T Street.

Shannon stopped about halfway down to point at a faded, wooden, stand-alone garage painted an incongruous shell pink. "That's hers."

Lexi grabbed the door handle and jerked it upward, discouraged by the thought that the door was probably locked and operated by a remote door opener stashed in Claudia's car. The door rose a foot or two, enough that she could see the trunk and tires of a red Honda HR-V.

"That's Claudia's," Shannon confirmed, ducking under the low garage door to inch into the garage like a fawn slipping through low hanging branches entering a forest. "Look." Shannon pointed to a bumper sticker reading LOCKE. "She's been down in the Delta by the river. If she went on vacation, her suitcase might be in the trunk."

Lexi's heart thudded. She had seen trunks opened on *Law and Order* and last week on a *The Closer* re-run. She could picture what might lie waiting. Or who. Was it Claudia?

Shannon walked around, peering into the car. "There's nobody in here."

"Oh?"

"Daddy opens things with one of these." Shannon lifted a metal tool from where it leaned against the wall. "It's called a crowbar, but it has nothing to do with crows. Words are weird, aren't they?"

"Yes," Lexi thought, flashing on the scenes when the car trunk opened in the media. "Shannon, that's probably dirty."

"No, it's shiny clean."

She studied Shannon with her freckled face—a child, innocent, pet-loving, young enough to find adventure with dear Nancy Drew. Would a sharp encounter with reality ruin books for her?

Shannon shoved the crowbar into the line where the trunk closed, an act that should have been Lexi's if she weren't such a weakling, she thought.

Lexi closed her eyes to the blue-jeaned legs she saw folded in the trunk. Softly, she said, "It looks like we've found Claudia." She lifted the trunk lid fully open.

"No!" Shannon's reply was loud and firm. "This is Jimmy." He looked like a man taking a nap in the trunk, except for the bashed skull. Shannon said, "I guess he's keeping ravens busy down in hell, not in Locke. He shouldn't have been mean to Claudia. You think fate struck him down for that? Get down, Cosmo."

She pushed the cat from the bumper, engendering a low growl. Tangerine jumped into Cosmo's place. "Are you calling the police, Lexi? We still don't know where Claudia is."

Lexi nodded. She had already punched in 9-1-1. She gave her information, then clicked her phone off. "Who is 'we'?" she asked.

"You and me," Shannon answered. "Who else would it be?"

Lexi grinned. "You and me and Cosmo and Tangerine."

The two cats stood at the front of the garage, staring at the side door.

Shannon was quick to grasp Lexi's point. "Shall I open it?"

"No, let's wait," Lexi answered. Outside, she heard tires rolling up and then car doors slamming and distant radio voices. In front of her, Cosmo meowed a welcome as the side door opened. Claudia and the Sacramento police entered at the same time.

"Jimmy's napping," Shannon explained to perplexed officers.

STARKRIMSON

Darrell Vaughn Smith

She followed the low howl through the pear orchards to the edge of the property, steam from her breath leading the way, her shoes sinking into the loam. The howl, closer now, changed to a clipped yelp before returning to another agonized moan, then nothing but the steady roar of the Sacramento River in the distance.

The bough shone wetly in the flashlight's glare. A beam briefly caught the pears' gleaming flesh. The blood-red fruit hung heavy in the trees like an omen. She looked down, sank to her knees and screamed.

Her phone rang.

"Baby, where are you?"

"Granddad, it's Rocket. He's…" and she screamed again.

"I know. I found one of the calves in the driveway. Stay there. Keep your phone on. Can you do that for me? I'm on my way."

Two words scrawled in the newling's blood seeped into the garage's heavy, wooden door.

Get out.

***

It had never been easy. Clarks had owned this land since the end of the Pacific War. Sgt. Solomon Clark was a Montford Point Marine, one of the Marines' first Black recruits, fought in Saipan and Guam. He took his wife and baby boy, Bronze

Star, and life savings from Detroit to California and bought sixty acres of river mud along the Sacramento. He signed the deed in his dress blues and battled the white farmers every step of the way, defending every inch of Sacramento River soil as he did the Saipan sand. The old Marine fought them off with an M-1 rifle back in the day.

But the rules of engagement changed. They didn't burn crosses anymore. They hired expensive Los Angeles lawyers dressed in Savile Row suits.

Solomon Coleridge Clark III wore his Sunday suit on a Tuesday morning, ready to fight another day for his family's land. His granddaughter Tephaney drove the truck up the river road to the Sacramento County courthouse.

They sat silently side by side in the cramped cab as the NPR news reader talked about the latest effort to send Delta water to the Southland before teasing the story of a Sacramento developer's dream to turn the Delta into the California Riviera. Tephaney Clark slowly shook her head behind the wheel.

The message has never changed.

Get out.

***

Dana Hawkins walked down the fifth-floor corridor of the old downtown courthouse to the trio at the end of the hall. He wore a reporter's sport coat, bow tie and dark slacks—a holdover from his days on the beat. His footsteps echoed off the checkerboard marble tile, the floor quiet after the noon recess cleared the courtrooms.

Three stone-faced white men wearing matching dark blue suits, their hair varied shades of gray strode past. The last of the lawyers trailing slightly behind gave Hawkins a quick side-eye.

Henry Childs waved Hawkins over. Hank and Hawk went back years. The old counselor opened his civil practice about the same time Hawkins hired on at the downtown news. That seemed a lifetime ago now, before the layoffs, before they bulldozed the daily to make way for condos.

He'd worked twenty-seven years there. Sports first, nightside cops, then the courthouse where he first met Childs. He was babysitting jurors' deliberations when he got the call to come back to the shop. The bosses were waiting with his separation papers. The whole thing took 15 minutes. Childs was his first call as he walked across the parking lot. That was three years ago.

Childs slipped him some PI work now and then, fraud cases, personal injury. The checks kept the lights on and gave Hawk a little running money.

But this case was different. All Hawkins needed to see were the photos of the Clarks' driveway.

"We're not going anywhere. Clarks have grown pears on this land since after the war. Starkrimson and Red d'Anjou. Our pears were served at the White House. They're in every store and restaurant for a hundred miles. DeBoer's LA lawyers aren't pushing us out, and the next time I'm hosing blood off my driveway, it won't be my livestock's. Bet on that."

Hawkins walked up as Solomon Clark finished the sentence. Solomon looked about seventy but had a solid, compact build like a catcher back when the big leagues had Black catchers. Campy or John Roseboro or Elston Howard.

Childs was about to introduce the two, "Dana, this is…" but Clark stepped on the line. He stuck out a catcher's mitt palm. "Solomon Coleridge Clark. Named after my father and his father before him. Over here's my granddaughter Tephaney."

Tephaney Clark, dressed in an indigo suit and matching low heels, carried the same compact build but stood slightly taller than her father. The cart behind her topped with exhibits and legal documents gave her the look of Childs' co-counsel. Tephaney managed a tight smile and a curt "Mr. Hawkins."

She'd found the family dog in the pear orchard.

"These last few days have been ... We shouldn't have to be in a court of law proving we own the land that's been ours for eighty years. Now, the governor wants to dig tunnels through it. Then what they did to Rocket and to our home. Our home. They killed my dog. My granddaddy's right. Next blood we wash away won't be calf's blood." Clark's granddaughter paused. "I'm afraid of what he might do."

Childs looked uneasily down the courthouse corridor and caught Hawkins' eye.

"We can't worry about the governor. But we're going to find out who's behind what happened at your place. That's why Mr. Hawkins is here. Right now, we've got to focus on this case. Court reconvenes in fifteen. I'll meet you and Mr. Clark back in the courtroom."

***

Forty-eight minutes later, Hawkins' Buick Electra rolled up the gravel road to the DeBoer Family Dairy & Creamery. A flotilla of cream-colored trucks emblazoned on each side with the DeBoer name idled in a nearby lot as blue-uniformed workers loaded in hand trucks of milk, butter, and eggs.

A bald, blue-suited security guard built like a defensive end stood in the middle of the road between the Buick and the dairy's entrance.

"Can I help you? You look lost, son," the red-faced guard said stonily. "Clark Farms is just up the road. You must've missed it."

"I know exactly where I am. And you look like you've had too much sun. Let's get you some shade." Hawkins looked down at No-Neck's name badge. "Kevin."

Hawkins climbed out of the Buick. Kevin placed his hand over his holster.

"Easy, Kevin. You're starting to sweat. Dana Hawkins. I'm here to see Willy DeBoer. No, he's not expecting me. I just have a few questions and I'll be out of your hair."

An electric motor whirred behind them as DeBoer pulled his golf cart beside the sentry shack.

"Thank you, Kevin. I'll take it from here," then to Hawkins, "Willy DeBoer. Make it quick."

DeBoer wore a long-sleeve shirt in a tiny checkerboard print, canvas pants and Mackintoshes. His jowly face and ruddy cheeks gave him the look of Bob's Big Boy come to life.

Hawkins introduced himself and handed DeBoer a short stack of snapshots from the orchard and the slaughter in the Clarks' driveway. DeBoer flipped through them and winced slightly before handing them back.

"Sick business, but you're off base if you're insinuating we had anything to do with this. Probably some drugged-out kids. They probably put it all on TikTok."

"There's no love lost between you two. You sued Clark Farms. There was a hearing today?"

"As my bank account is quite aware, Mr. Harvey. Those LA fellows don't come cheap."

"Hawkins."

DeBoer ignored him.

"Believe me, we didn't want it to come to this. Lawyers, courtrooms, legal fees. We both have businesses to run. But we believe that orchard land along the river belongs to us. We assured Clark we would even pay fair market value for it, but we couldn't reason with him. He was so angry. You people are always flying off into a rage about something. All that rage. Why is that Mr. Hawkins?"

Hawkins didn't take the bait.

"You'll let me know if you hear anything?" he said and handed him a business card.

DeBoer smiled and tore the card in half.

"Now, why would I do that, Mr. Hawkins? See you in court."

***

The phone's ring jolted Hawkins out of a heavy, dreamless sleep. Hours still before sunrise. He grabbed the cell off the nightstand on the second ring.

"Yeah."

"DeBoer's dead. They think Granddad did it. Sheriffs just took him downt…"

Tephaney was shouting into the phone, the words pouring out rapid-fire.

"Dead? Slow down. Call Childs. Tell him to get to the Sheriff's Office. I'll meet you there."

Childs drove to the H Street headquarters in record time. He was heading to meet Clark in interrogation when Tephaney and Hawkins met him at the entrance's double glass doors.

"They say DeBoer was gunned down by a high-powered rifle. Two shots from distance, from the direction of Clark Farms. They found him in his cab in the truck lot. I'm heading to the interview room now."

"That's nonsense. My grandfather would never kill a man. Look, the DeBoers have been trying to push us off our land since we set foot on it. They're low down. Willy's the worst of them. But Granddad didn't do this."

Childs turned to Hawkins. "They're going to want to talk to you, too. You were one of the last people to see DeBoer alive. I'm representing you now. We'll go over how that went down, and I'll be in the box with you."

"Nothing to go over, Hank. Security officer was a dick. Ol' Kevin treated that dairy like it was Fort Knox. DeBoer all but spit in my face."

"And now he's dead," Tephaney said.

A gray-haired man, his face the color of oatmeal, his suit the same shade, was also in the lobby. The man's eyes shifted ever so quickly to the three before he disappeared down a corridor.

Hawkins was sure he'd seen him before.

***

Childs opened the door to the Spartan interrogation room, and Hawkins followed behind. Clark was seated behind the table. He was still wearing his bedclothes and sheriff-issue shower tongs.

"Don't say a word, Mr. Clark," Childs said.

Detective Sergeant Dobbins was working solo.

"Hey, Hank," Dobbins said. "Thought you practiced civil. Family discount?"

Childs deflected the barb and landed one of his own.

"Off the Brady list, yet, Dob?"

Dobbins smirked, but Hawkins knew the question stung. Dobbins was busted a couple years back for lying on the stand. Hawkins broke the story.

"Hey, Hawkins? Didn't the daily fishwrap let you go? How's the job search?"

"Your wife says it's going just fine."

"You Black sonofa..." Dobbins lunged at Hawkins, but Childs stepped in between as Dobbins and Hawkins glared at each other.

Lt. Braccia stepped out from behind the one-way mirror that looked into the interview room.

"Is there a problem, Detective?" Braccia surveyed the room. "Maybe it's time Harris gave you a break."

"We're good, lieutenant." Braccia shut the door behind him.

"Do you have any questions for me, sergeant?" Clark said. "Because you've wasted enough of my time."

"You're a hunter, Mr. Clark. You must know your way around a rifle. Coroner's got DeBoer on a slab right now. We'll be testing the ballistics on those rounds." Dobbins pulled out a small notebook.

"And you were overheard at the courthouse saying something about hosing someone else's blood off of your driveway. Is that correct? Oh, and sorry about the calf."

Clark rose from the table. Childs laid a hand on his shoulder.

"Hey," Dobbins raised his hands in surrender. "I get it. I'm from Galt. I was in FFA. Those calves get to be like family, am I right?"

"Any leads on my client's case?"

"The dog's name was 'Rocket,' right?" Dobbins, pushing another emotional button. We've got our best men on it. Working 'round the clock."

"Are we done, Detective?"

"For now, Mr. Childs. But you tell your friend Mr. Clark here to stay close. That goes for Dana Hawkins, too."

"I didn't kill that man, Counselor. But give me five minutes with that, Dobbins," Clark said as the two walked back to Childs' car.

Clark stopped abruptly and turned to Childs.

"You know, there's not too many of us Black growers left out here—I can just about count 'em on one hand. But we've done it for damn near eighty years. Eighty years. Tephaney's going to run all of this someday. She graduated with honors from NC A&T, a master's from Tuskegee. She could take over today if the time came. Point is, the DeBoers are a miserable bunch, they've had nothing but hate for us ever since we got here, but I'll be damned if I'd risk everything we built to kill Willy DeBoer's sorry ass."

"I know."

"But I won't be responsible for what happens to whoever did this to us."

"I know that, too."

***

Daybreak and the television trucks were already lined up along the road leading to Clark Farms. The reporters' scrum, all cameras, tripods, and microphones, blocked the entrance, where Calista DeBoer held court behind sunglasses from a small wooden podium. Her strawberry-blonde hair was pulled away from her face and held with a chunky white clip. A white cotton jacket and matching capris completed the outfit. She looked like someone who could get in nine holes before going to work.

"The DeBoer family and all who knew Willy are devastated by this heinous act that so savagely ended my husband's life. Willy was a good, decent, honorable man who loved his family, his Lord, his community, and the family dairy and creamery that brought smiles and endless memories to the Sacramento area for more than a century," she said.

DeBoer dabbed at tears behind her shades, then set her gaze at the wall of cameras.

"I'm standing here, not at my family's home, but here at the home of the man who killed my husband." Cameras flashed and whirred in rapid-fire rhythm. "Solomon Clark is not yet under arrest for his brutality, but neither I nor the DeBoer family will rest until he is made to pay for what he's done. Our families have had their differences over the years, but we are sickened by…"

The herd of reporters turned and swarmed Childs' car. Clark looked out at the chaos from the passenger side window, the reporters' shouted questions muffled by the glass.

"Mr. Clark. Ready?" Childs said as he brought the car to a stop at the Clarks' doorstep. They opened the car doors to the reporters' barrage. Childs shouted over the din.

"No questions."

***

"Lord, have mercy. Brandy?" Clark sighed and reached for the den's bar. The lack of sleep and the scene outside added years to his face.

"A little early," Hawkins answered. The wall clock read 8:50 a.m. "Coffee?"

"Suit yourself."

Childs and Tephaney Clark sat opposite each other in the darkened den, watching a replay of Calista DeBoer's sunrise press conference like game film. Tephaney scribbled notes on a yellow legal pad as the DeBoer wife's voice shouted from the flat screen.

Hawkins walked back in from the kitchen. "Hey, Hank. Pause that."

Calista DeBoer froze in mid-sentence. To her right, a sad-looking man in a gray suit was also trapped in time.

"Him."

"The creepy guy from sheriff's headquarters?" Tephaney answered.

"And the courthouse. Only he was wearing blue. Gave me the side eye when he walked by with the other two suits he was with."

"Frank Whelan. Dunaway-Whelan," Childs said. "High-dollar Capitol Mall law firm, half the developers in town have them on retainer. D.W. lobbies for the other half. So, why the ringside seat?"

"Let's find out."

Hawkins was back on the river road to Sacramento. He rolled down the driver's side window, letting the rush of Delta air clear his head of the long night and the chaotic morning. But thoughts of the sad man in the gray suit returned.

Whelan at the courthouse. Whelan at Sheriff's headquarters. Now today at Clark Farms with a front row seat to Callie DeBoer's stunt. What's the connection to the DeBoers?

Hawkins stopped by his downtown walk-up, grabbed a clean suit and headed to the Capitol Mall offices of Dunaway-Whelan.

The heavy brushed steel doors that greeted Hawkins on the 23rd floor gave the offices an aura of impenetrability, but they opened as easily as any other. The disinterested millennial at reception looked over the top of his cosmetic glasses and raised an index finger.

"Dunaway-Whelan. Please hold."

Then to Hawkins: "We didn't order DoorDash."

Hawkins leaned over the reception desk.

"Try again."

"May I help you?"

"Better. Frank Whelan."

"And may I ask…"

"You may not. Tell Mr. Whelan I'm a friend of Solomon Clark."

Hawkins looked down to the glass walled conference room at the end of the hall.

Milos Kanakaredes waved his hands dramatically in front of a large video screen as a row of men and women in matching suits sat rapt. Hawkins knew Milos for his string of downtown developments—and his flamboyant, take-no-prisoners dealmaking. An animation showed plans for his latest dream project, the one all over the news, Destination Delta.

"We don't normally speak to the friends of murderers, but I felt I should make an exception. Please." Whelan motioned Hawkins to his office, his sad, gray expression unchanged.

"I'm good. You know damn well Clark didn't kill DeBoer. You also seem to be spending a lot of time around the Clarks. The courthouse, the middle of the night at Sheriff's headquarters, and beside Ms. DeBoer in front of the Clark home this morning. Three times in less than forty-eight hours."

"I guess this makes it four. Dunaway-Whelan is one of the largest firms on the West Coast. Of course, we have business before the court. It was a mere coincidence that we were on your floor when we heard Mr. Clark's unfortunate outburst. His words, sadly, seem a bit prescient now. Thankfully, we were able to relay that to the authorities. Sheriff's Detective Dobbins has been especially helpful."

"And Kanakaredes?"'

"Milos' dream of developing the Delta is no secret. Why, it's all over the news. He is a valued client, and we're happy to provide any services he requires. The DeBoers are a Sacramento institution. We at Dunaway-Whelan have a deep relationship with the family, and were, understandably, shocked at Willy's untimely death," Whelan purred.

"We were ready to provide any support Calista needed. Of course, we had no control over the venue—or the manner —in which she chose to express her grief. We can only hope, as I'm sure she does, that justice is served. Now, if you'll excuse me, these men will show you out."

Two black-suited heavies with UFC builds clutched Hawkins' arms. Hawkins shook them off and took three quick punches to the gut for his trouble. Hawkins coughed, groaned, but stayed on his feet.

"And if you show up at our door again, Mr. Hawkins, next time, they won't use the elevator."

Hawkins walked around his Buick in a quick inspection, then eased himself inside and took inventory. Bruises but nothing broken. He'll be sore tomorrow. He was sore now, pissed that he let Whalen's goons get the drop on him.

His phone buzzed inside his hip pocket.

"Hawkins."

"Hawk, it's Clark. Get back to the farm. A van just rolled by and shot up the place. I got some shots off, but none that did any damage. We're OK, but my granddaughter's a little shaken up. And, be careful. Watch yourself. They're coming for us."

Hawkins pulled off the Capitol Mall curb, making sure he didn't pick up a tail. He stuck to surface streets and found Freeport Boulevard onto Route 160.

The drive to Clark Farms was quick. He checked the rear-view one last time before turning onto the driveway. Bullet holes riddled the front of the house and the garage door where a threat had been scrawled in blood a couple of nights earlier.

Clark met Hawkins at the front door and reassured him that everyone was all right. He was keeping the cops out of it for now, which meant it would be a while before a news crew picked up on it. Clark looked him up and down.

"Looks like you got what you were looking for from that lawyer and then some. Tephaney did some more digging after you left.

"Come inside. I'll let her tell you the rest. I'm going to clean up this mess."

Tephaney had moved her notes onto the dining room table.

"So, before we were nearly killed, I found some documents that show both Dunaway-Whelan and Kanakaredes are big donors to, you guessed it, the Calista DeBoer Family Foundation. They've given millions. Kanakaredes made a big show of it at the foundation's awards gala."

She showed images from the developer's website: The DeBoers and Kanakaredes smiling and holding a giant cardboard check. The DeBoers in gala finery.

"And I saw this." She expanded an image, then zoomed in on a face. Detective Dobbins. "I called a friend. She interns at the foundation. Said it was an open secret that Mrs. DeBoer was having dinner with Willy at home and some cop for dessert. That it was just fun gossip until the other night."

"So, Dobbins is running the murder investigation of his lover's husband. Whelan overhears your grandfather in the courthouse and feeds that to him, and now he's Dobbins' prime suspect. Whelan works for Kanakaredes, who is bankrolling Calista DeBoer's foundation, and now Milos wants a return on his investment."

"But we weren't giving in," Clark said. "And when we went to court, they needed a plan B to get me out of the picture."

"And Willy DeBoer." Hawkins paused, running through his mental checklist. Clark picked up on it.

"What're you thinking?"

"Mr. Clark, you haven't called the cops yet. Think you can dig a couple shell fragments out of that wall over there? Childs, you still have a man in ballistics, right? Tell him to pull the rounds from DeBoer's murder and compare them with the ones you're about to drive over there. Tell him to keep it quiet. Then call Dobbins and DeBoer's reps. Tell them your client's ready to turn himself in. I'll call Lt. Braccia. It's a gamble, but I think my hunch is right."

***

The Clarks, Childs and Hawkins walked over to the wide interrogation table across from Detective Dobbins at Sheriff's headquarters. Clark, dressed in his Sunday suit, sat first.

"You're doing the right thing, Mr.Clark," Dobbins said, trying for an empathetic tone.

"I just feel I need to do this. There's been so much pain."

"Before we begin," Childs said, "my office has conducted our own investigation into Willy DeBoer's homicide—and incidents that happened at Clark Farms prior to and after his death. The vandalism and animal cruelty, the two shots that killed DeBoer, and, just yesterday, an unreported shooting into the Clarks' home from the river road. We've determined the rounds match, but they weren't fired from any of Mr. Clark's weapons. Indeed, they were fired from a weapon similar to those stored at the sheriff's armory."

Dobbins stood up and pushed the metal chair back, color rising over his collar.

"What're you getting at?"

"The rounds were fired from a service weapon, detective. A weapon you checked out, by our records, at least three times. But three times was enough, wasn't it, detective? Sit down. There's more. We were able to review security camera footage from that first terrible night at Clark Farms," Childs said, fanning out photos in front of Dobbins.

"Driving away from the scene was a dark Ford Econoline van. The same van seen near the DeBoer dairy before Willy was shot, the same van that took potshots at my client's home yesterday afternoon, and the same unmarked van that undercover deputies use on stakeouts. You killed DeBoer. You threatened and tried to kill Clark and his granddaughter. Who put you up to it?"

Dobbins slammed the table with both hands.

"Make me a deal, and I'll tell you everything."

The interrogation room door flew open.

"You coward," Calista DeBoer shouted. She and Lt. Braccia were watching from behind the one-way glass. "Shut up."

"It's too late, Callie. I'm not going down for this alone."

"Fine," she hissed. "DeBoer's was always Willy's show. 'Bringing smiles to Sacramento.' All that, 'We started our dairy with fifty dollars and our mama's two cows in Courtland,' song-and-dance. But I was the one running it, and I was done. I wanted out. I begged Willy to sell, but he wasn't having it. Then Kanakaredes started waving money around. We had lunch before my foundation's gala, and he showed me his plan for the Delta. Hotels, docks, four-star resorts, said to consider his donation to my foundation a down payment—if I could chase the Clarks off their land and get Willy to sign off on a sale. Can I smoke?"

Hawkins tossed over a pack of Winstons. She looked at the pack, "Any port in a storm," she said and lit up.

"But that sonofabitch just couldn't help himself. He had to go and sue for that orchard land by the river. As much as he hated you, he wanted that land that much more. But a court trial wasn't on my timeline. I needed help. Milos suggested Johnny Law over there. Said he's been on the Kanakaredes payroll for years. He's a dirty cop, so I knew I could count on him. All I had to do was unbutton a button or two, show a little leg. It was easier than I thought. I was almost flattered."

"Go to hell," Dobbins shouted.

"We're already there, sweetie. You Clarks weren't going to sell after the mess ol' Dob made of your property—I did not expect him to go after the animals. That's on me. The hell is wrong with you, Lyle. But a murder rap might force your hand. And Willy's widow, too grief-stricken to carry on, would have to sell the family business..."

"To Kanakaredes." Tephaney shook her head. "You are one sick..."

The widow DeBoer stared unblinking at her and flicked an ash on the floor.

Lt. Braccia walked out from behind the one-way glass. Two uniformed deputies met him at the door.

"Sgt. Lyle Dobbins, you are under arrest for the murder of Willy DeBoer and for the attempted murders of Solomon

Clark, Tephaney Clark, and Henry Childs. Anything you say can and will be used against you. Calista DeBoer, I place you under arrest for solicitation to commit murder for the murder of Willy DeBoer. Anything you say can or will be..."

Hawkins nodded, and the Clarks and Childs rose as one and headed for the lobby.

"Hank and Hawk, we make a pretty good team," Childs said, clapping Hawkins on the shoulder.

Tephaney embraced each of the men in turn.

"You saved my grandfather's life. Thank you."

She reached out to her grandfather. They hugged for a long time, Tephaney feeling like a child again in his arms.

"We're not going anywhere," he said, finally. "Bet on that."

FOWL PLAY

Linda Joy Singleton

"I'm going to kill them!" Grandma exclaimed, stomping mud from her boots as she stormed up the steps to the farmhouse. "I want every last one of those thieving varmints dead!"

I jumped off the porch swing, tossing aside the Agatha Christie novel (The Murder of Roger Ackroyd) I was a chapter away from finishing. Mom, my brother, and I had only lived at my grandmother's farm in Galt for a week, but that was long enough to know the bucking-bronco ride of Grandma's temper.

"What happened?" I asked although I could guess the answer. Last week, a Sussex chicken disappeared during the night. Grandma blamed coyotes.

"Three Swedish Black chicks gone! My poor featherbabies." Blinking away tears, Grandma kicked off her muddy boots, her sun-weathered face red with fury. Neighbors in this rural area nicknamed her "Bird Lady" because she raised a menagerie of peacocks, emus, ducks, chickens, and turkeys. She wasn't the stereotypical sweet old lady—she was hard as a bullet with a gaze that could pierce through steel. Mom often teased that Grandma cared more about her birds than her family.

"Don't just stand there like a fence post, Stacia!" Grandma snapped. "Get your mother while I load my gun. I'm going to track down those killers and—" She stopped abruptly at the creak of an opening door.

Mom yawned as she came over, buttoning her pink fuzzy robe. She took one look at Grandma and sighed. "More missing birds?"

"Three very valuable Swedish Black chicks—a breed that will lay eggs even in the winter." Grandma swore, her expression darker than storm clouds. "I spotted coyote prints nearby. They're not getting away with it this time. I'm going after them."

"No, Mama. You're doing no such thing." Mom put her arm gently around Grandma. "You can't walk without limping."

"I may not move fast with my bad hip, but I can still shoot straight."

While Mom tried to calm Grandma, I stood back watching. My tangled emotions were as prickly as wild vines. I should feel sad or maybe guilty, but all I felt was bitterness and anger at my family. I did not want to be here. I wanted to enjoy summer by swimming, biking, and playing games with my friends. Instead, I'd been forced to leave civilization to live on a run-down farm at the edge of Sacramento County. Mom said country life would be good for us. But by "us," she meant my younger brother Jarod. After Mom and Dad separated, Jarod started hanging out with some rough kids and was arrested for vandalism. He'd probably still be behind bars if he hadn't been a first-time offender and only thirteen.

But I was an A student (except for a B in algebra), did my chores without complaining (much), and hadn't done anything wrong (at least nothing they knew about). So, why was I being punished, too?

Mom managed to calm Grandma down by promising to find a non-violent plan to protect the birds.

"All right, we'll do it your way," Grandma agreed reluctantly. "But if that doesn't work, I'm going to kill those killers."

And I knew she meant it.

***

Mom contacted a local animal rights group and borrowed a huge cage. Her "great plan" was to trap each coyote and relocate them to the foothills. Not easy since new homes were sprouting up like weeds, pushing wild creatures out of their habitat. I couldn't help but feel sorry for them. I knew what it was like to be forced out of my home. I missed my friends SO much and couldn't even text with them until I could afford to replace my broken cell phone.

Still, I was relieved that no animals would be hurt in this plan, and I pushed all thoughts of coyotes and missing chickens from my mind.

That evening, while I was washing dishes, my brother came up beside me with an odd look on his face. "What if the coyotes didn't do it?"

"Didn't do what?" I pretended not to understand, hoping he'd go away. I did not want to talk about this—especially with the person responsible for ruining my summer.

"Didn't kill the chicks." A strand of hay poked up in his curly black hair, but I didn't tell him. I turned back to the sink to continue washing dishes.

"Seriously, Stacia." Jarod grasped my arm, turning me to face him. "I've been helping the farmhands with the livestock and noticed something suspicious."

"Suspicious?" I dropped a dish into the gray water, soapy bubbles splashing my face.

"Dan—the short guy with a beard—suddenly has an expensive new watch. And Michelle—she works out a lot and can lift barrels without sweating—complained about how expensive her gym is, so she could use the extra money.

Remember what Gran said about the chicks being valuable?" my bother rushed on excitedly. "What if Dan or Michelle stole the chicks and sold them for lots of money?"

I wiped soap from my face and stared at my brother. "This isn't a mystery and you're not Sherlock Holmes."

"But I didn't see any tiny feathers either," he pointed out. "And when I saw the coyote prints Grandma mentioned, they were dried up, not recent."

"Since when do you know anything about animal prints?"

He drew back like my words slapped him. "Not much else to do after morning chores ... so I've been reading some books...learning about working on a farm. I know you hate being here...but I don't. It's peaceful and no one is pressuring me. I like being with Grandma, too. I want to help her."

"You can help by not turning something natural into a mystery. Coyotes kill chickens. It happens. Now leave me alone."

Excitement drained from his face, and he swore something really mean at me, then stomped out of the room. I almost felt guilty...almost.

The trap was found empty in the morning. The coyotes weren't easily tricked. And they were clever enough to stay away. No more birds went missing.

But on the next night, we all awoke to frantic yapping.

Mom, Grandma, Jarod, and I dressed quickly and then rushed out to check the trap. We found a large tawny-gray coyote snarling and pacing inside the cage.

Mom was triumphant. Grandma was thrilled. Jarod stared like he'd never seen a wild animal up close. And I didn't say anything either. I was just glad all the drama about coyotes and missing chickens would end soon.

After we'd returned to bed, and even the caged coyote stopped yapping, I woke up again. What was that sound? An odd shuffling-like footsteps. When I peeked out of my bedroom, I saw a shadowy figure tip-toeing down the hall. I recognized my brother's lanky shape and long stride.

Why was Jarod sneaking around? There wasn't a mystery for him to solve. So what if the farmhands had a motive for stealing valuable birds? There was no evidence against them—only my brother's over-active imagination. Even Sherlock Jarod had to accept the fact that coyotes are predators. It's natural for them to attack birds—end of mystery.

Still, I'd better keep an eye on him or his curiosity could cause more trouble. Quickly, I slipped into jeans and a sweatshirt. When I put on my faded cowgirl boots, I scowled. My friends didn't wear their mothers' hand-me-downs. Of course, my friends weren't around to see me, and I couldn't post selfies with a broken phone. So, I grabbed a flashlight and shined the bright beam down the hall as I hurried outside.

Curiosity shifted to confusion when I spotted Jarod near the chicken coop. What was my brother doing? Was he up to no-good, like when he set off illegal fireworks or smashed mailboxes with his friends? I didn't think so. Being arrested had changed him. He wasn't rude and mean anymore, and he liked working with the livestock. It was almost as if we'd reversed roles—he was the good kid now.

So why sneak out?

A twig crunched under my boots, and I froze in place, my heart racing. He kept going, and I continued following. He passed the chicken coop, heading for the dark shadow of the barn.

A light atop the peaked roof shone on my brother as he slipped into the building. Despite the warm summer weather, I shivered. Not because I was cold but because I was worried. Jared had recently changed so much that Mom was talking about returning home next week. But if my brother caused any trouble, we might be stuck here all summer.

Creeping up to the barn, I cracked open the door and peered inside. Jared turned on a flashlight as he headed for the back corner to the cage where the coyote's yellow eyes gleamed suspiciously.

Suspicion rose in me, too. I didn't trust the coyote or my brother. Jared and I used to be close, but we drifted apart as we hung out with different friends. I blamed him for my parents' arguments, Mom missing so much work she lost her job, and for our banishment to a farm that felt like a prison to me.

Jared knelt beside the coyote cage, which caused the wild creature to hunch low with barred teeth and narrowed yellow eyes.

"It's okay, fella. I know how you feel," I heard Jared whisper. And then to my shock, my brother pulled a slice of bologna from his pocket and inched his hand close to the cage-

"No!" I shouted, bursting out of the darkness. "Jared, are you insane? He'll bite your fingers right off. Chomp! Juicy Jared finger-snacks."

"What are you doing here?" he demanded.

"Making sure you don't do anything dumb."

"Too late. Just leave." He pursed his lips, guilty-like.

"Why?"

"None of your business. Go away."

"Not until I know what you're planning."

"Geez, you're a jerk." He glanced at the coyote, frowned, then faced me. "Okay, you wanna know? I'm gonna let the coyote go free. He's got a right to live his own life."

"Why do you care?"

"I just do." He was silent; shoulders slumped but his mouth set determinedly.

I turned back to the coyote. He almost looked like an ordinary dog—until he lifted his head and captured my gaze. The world seemed to pause. I stared into his lonely, wild eyes.

All I could hear was the beat-beat of my heart. But I felt something more; a deep communication that cut through skin and bone to my soul.

Jarod was right, I realized. The coyote didn't belong in a cage. Still, I was surprised that Jared cared so much. Since Dad left, my brother acted like he didn't care about anything. This was a new side of my brother, and I was glad—not just for the coyote, but because Jared wasn't going to cause trouble for me.

He was going to help.

I didn't stick around to watch the coyote's release. I had other things to do, and fortunately Jared was too busy to notice.

See, being in high school isn't easy, especially when you can't afford nice things. I was furious when Mom refused to buy a new phone for me, so I saved money to buy it myself. I'd only earned half of what I'd needed from baby-sitting before moving here.

Babysitting doesn't pay much—but selling valuable chicks does—fifty to a hundred bucks per chick. I'd hid them in a small shed that no one used, sneaking out to give them food and water, waiting for a chance to sell them.

When the chicks vanished, everyone assumed a coyote did it, just like they would assume the coyote broke free on his own.

But something changed in me when I peered into the coyote's eyes. Being dishonest was like putting my soul in a cage. I guess my real friends would have to learn to like me, even if I couldn't afford a new phone.

I hoped they would.

The next morning, my family was surprised to find the coyote missing. But the biggest surprise was when they went into the chicken coop and found that the three missing chicks had returned.

Everyone was mystified ... except me.
And the coyote roamed free.

DEATH OF AN UGLY WOMAN

William Bishop

"Good morning. May I help you?" the girl asked.

Munroe found himself looking at a girl … make that a young woman. A fresh, unblemished face, light touch of make-up. She was smiling up at him, graciously eager to be of assistance. Innocent. He held out his badge wallet. A gold detective's badge and ID. Held it out where she could examine it.

"Detective Munroe, Sacramento Police. I need to speak with Mr. Peters. I believe he's the general manager here?"

"Yes, sir. Mr. Peters, that's correct. May I tell him what this is about?" A pleasant lilt to the voice.

"We've received a missing persons report. I'm looking into it."

"If you'll have a seat, I'll just let Mr. Peters know you're here."

It was a small reception lobby, a single desk, and four chairs, two each against the side walls. On each wall, a large painting depicted an artist's perception of a tomato. Munroe thought rendering might be a better word. The tomato, rendered. He decided he'd never understand modern art. Munroe took the first empty chair. A low fence separated the lobby from an open-plan office, where two columns of desks receded to a back wall. The quiet hum of business filled the air as the receptionist discretely murmured into her telephone. Looked up again at him. Smiled.

"Mr. Peters will be right out."

"Right out" proved to be a couple of minutes. Munroe noted the man was shorter than he expected. Charles Peters was pushing beyond the limits of middle age, sporting the belly that came with it. Strands of dark, oiled hair were carefully arrayed over a pink and otherwise bald dome.

"Detective Munroe. I'm Charles Peters." His voice boomed with bonhomie as his hand reached out to be shaken. "Come on back," he continued. "We can talk in my office."

His office appeared to be a photo gallery. Wherever walls lacked windows, framed photographs took their place—trucks dumped tomatoes into water-filled vats. Elevators lifted acres of tomatoes up to overhead sluices. Enormous stainless-steel cookers filled the processing hall with steam. A framed photograph on the far end of a large desk was totally at odds with the others—Peters and a woman, a young man between them. Munroe made the boy's age at nineteen or twenty. The woman had a pleasant face, a wash of freckles across her nose and short blond hair.

"Have a seat." Peters moved around behind the desk to take his place on a swiveling leather throne. "So, tell me, what brings one of Sacramento's finest to our humble processing plant?"

"As your girl probably told you, I'm looking into a missing persons report. Brenda Edwards. I'm told she works here, so I thought I'd start with some background."

"Jesus! Brenda? She's my office manager. I wondered why she didn't come to work this morning. Jennifer said she didn't even call in—she's the girl you spoke to out front. And you say Brenda's missing."

Peters leaned back in his chair, a puzzled look on his face. "That's not good, not good. And you're trying to find her." He paused to shake his head. "That's not good at all!" He paused and looked concerned a bit longer. Then leaned forward.

His long-sleeved shirt was a crisp white and his arms were crossed on the desk before him. The pose of a manager who had dealt with the issue and was moving on.

Peters was shaking his head again. "Well, she's not here. As I just told you, she didn't come to work this morning. I don't know what more I can tell you."

"Her car is in the parking lot out front."

Peters deflated slightly. The issue was sticking around a bit longer. Sticking.

"It is? That's strange. No one's seen her today. Are you sure?"

Munroe checked his notes again.

"The plates match our records. Was she here yesterday?"

"She was. I think she might have left early, though, but I'm not sure."

"Would any of your staff know?"

"Let's go find out."

***

Stepping out of the office, Munroe faced a grid of six desks, six people busily at work, a light hum of conversation, someone on the phone, another two conferring. The underlying clatter of six keyboards as the office staff juggled the influx and outflow of tomatoes.

The man at the first desk was bone thin, skeletal, as old men sometimes are. What hair he had was white, the years of his life etched deeply in his face.

"Larry," Peters said. The man looked up from his computer, his face a living question mark. "This is Detective Munroe. He's asking about Brenda."

The man switched his attention to the detective. Still at a loss.

"Mr. Peters says Ms. Edwards was here yesterday," Munroe explained. "When was the last time you saw her?"

"The last time I saw her? Is she dead?" Larry's face brightened.

"She's been reported missing. That's all we know at the moment."

"Missing. Now how about that?" Larry relaxed back into his chair. "I wondered why I hadn't heard her today." Shook his head, smiling.

"Was she here yesterday?"

"Oh. Right. Yes, she was definitely here yesterday."

"When was the last time you saw her?" Munroe had his pen ready, his case folder open.

Hearing their conversation, a raw-boned woman at the next desk perked up, stopped working.

"I can't really say what time that was. It's like when you get a headache? You take an aspirin, but you never can say exactly when the headache goes away. Brenda's like that. But thinking about it now, I'd say things might've gotten normal here a little after one o'clock. I can't say I really noticed it until maybe one-thirty, two. Maybe a little later."

Munroe noted the man's distaste for Edwards.

"What you're saying, then, is that she might have left early yesterday."

"Yeah, most likely."

"But her car is still in the lot. Did she say anything to anyone about having car trouble?"

"Not that I heard."

"Could someone have given her a ride home, like maybe she got sick or something?"

"Let me put it this way." Larry smiled. "Say she had a one-way airplane ticket out of here, wanted a lift to the airport? We'd be stumbling over ourselves, trying to drive her there. Other than that? She's on her own."

Munroe noted that Peters remained unruffled by Larry's attitude toward Brenda.

"I sense you are not on good terms with Ms. Edwards."

"You could say that." Larry nodded, seeming to subject his conscience to a reality check. "Yes. Not on good terms. You know how it is, someone calls you Gramps when they're not related to you? How it is when they tell anyone who'll listen that you're useless, that you're ten years past your use-by date?" Larry was warming up now. "She was forever telling Charles he had to fire me. Telling me about the long line of people at the door she could replace me with. No, Detective, I was not on good terms with that."

Munroe made more notes in his book. Noted also none of this was news to Peters.

The woman from the next desk had stepped over to join the conversation. Gazed raptly at Peters.

"This is Janet Stokowski," Peters said. Indicating the detective, he explained "Janet, this is Detective Munroe, Sacramento Police Department."

"Officer," the woman nodded absently to him.

"It's Detective, ma'am."

"Sorry." She finally turned to Munroe. "I'm not going to say anything that Mr. Peters here doesn't know already. Brenda Edwards is not well-liked."

"She isn't pleasant, then. So, what is she like?"

"Well, I don't think I ever saw her smile. Sneer, yes. But not smile. She's just plain surly, is what she is. Like she didn't want to be here and didn't care who knew it. You definitely don't want to say anything she can interpret as a put-down. And that covers almost anything you might think of saying."

"And do you like her?" Munroe made more notes.

"When she goes around telling people I like other women? When she calls me the office dyke? Of course, I like her. Not."

"When was the last time you saw her?"

"That would be during lunch yesterday. She likes to bring her bucket of doom to lunch to share with everybody."

"Last seen at lunch break, then." More scribbling in his notebook.

"Yeah, I think so. I don't remember seeing her after that."

"Did she say anything about going anywhere?"

"She did say something about Jensen dropping trou in the back lot."

Munroe saw Peters wince at this last remark.

"I suspect she was planning on gifting him with her presence next."

"And Jensen is…"

"Our plant engineer," Peters explained. "He may still be in his office. I'll take you there."

Munroe noticed that the office had become significantly quieter, felt many eyes following him as Peters led the way to the back of the office and the door to the plant.

At the door, Peters paused.

"Jensen's likely out in the yard. We're adding a new color sorter, so Jensen is spending a few days out there taking measurements. We'll just have to see."

***

Munroe stepped through the door and into a wall of noise: the clatter of cans being chased down conveyors, the rumble of motors, the hissing of steam lines made normal conversation impossible. The temperature was already in the mid-nineties. Place a few enormous steam kettles in an enclosed processing hall and the workplace became a sauna. Munroe felt his shirt beginning to stick to him already. The air was heavy with the smell of cooking tomatoes. It wrapped itself around him, filling his nostrils, insinuating itself into the fabric of his clothing. He knew he would never be able to look at a bowl of tomato soup again.

Five yards in front of the detective, a broad conveyor carried a continuous river of tomatoes into the building, dropping them into what appeared to be a concrete containment bin, its walls about three feet high.

He pointed toward the structure. "What's that?"

"That's the hog. Come on, I'll show you."

Standing at the edge of the containment bin, Munroe leaned over to see a churning mass of red tomato pulp, skin, and juice, continually churning as more tomatoes were dumped in. Occasionally, a series of deadly-looking blades broke the surface as they rotated, ripping the tomatoes apart.

"Tomatoes come in here," Peters explained, "get pulped, and then piped on to the cookers." He gestured toward the large stainless-steel vessels farther in the building. They were still transfixed by the thrashing blades when Munroe turned to Peters.

"Doesn't look like it would be too hard to tip someone into this, does it?"

Peters looked at him blankly for a moment. "God damn it!"

He straightened abruptly. "Follow me," he commanded. Turning back the way they had come, he repeated himself. "God damn it!" Peters' face was becoming dangerously red.

***

The Security Department was a darkened shoe box of a room just off the front office. Two men sat at glowing monitors. Peters approached the first man.

"I want the feed from the number three camera. Don't put it on your screen."

The man began typing on his keyboard.

"Gimme yesterday's feed. Make it from, oh, let's say … 1:15 onward."

"You got it."

"And both of you," Peters continued. "Go take a cigarette break. I'll come get you when we're done."

Peters sat at the other monitor as the screen flickered, then bathed his face in phosphorescent light. A new black-and-white image appeared on the monitor.

Suddenly things became very quiet. Munroe pulled a chair over to watch. The video showed the back wall of the main office. A staircase to the left of the door rose up to a small landing at the second level. A closed door at the top, the only break in the otherwise blank wall. The hog was in full view in the foreground.

"Jesus," Peters mumbled. "Twenty hours and counting."

The video feed showed people walking into the frame, and then out again. A small box at the bottom of the screen showed time spooling up.

"Damn, damn, damn." Peters was still mumbling. The clock showed 1:20, and Peters slowed the display to real time. The two men waited, two pairs of eyes fixed on the monitor. Peters clicked the mouse rhythmically to bump the speed up momentarily. At 1:26, the back door opened. Peters let the video run normally as they watched a woman step through the doorway.

"OK, there's Brenda. Now..." Peters began to whistle softly through his teeth as the woman turned to her right and ascended the stairway. At the top, she opened the door and stepped inside. The door closed behind her.

"That's Jensen's office." Peters began to relax slightly. "Now let's see what happens."

The video continued to play on in real time. The upstairs door remained shut. Nothing seemed to be happening.

"I should explain. CalTom is a boutique cannery. We're not like Con Agra or Contadina; we're wholly owned by the Edwards family. You've probably noticed that Brenda is a living harassment lawsuit. She's unemployable. Her father put her here, ostensibly as office manager. She likes the title.

Everybody working here stays on because they need the job. The pay's good, very good, and that's because of her. The old man pays the price so he won't have to put up with her at home.

"I was wondering about that."

"Nobody likes her, but the extra salary bump makes it tolerable. Most of the time."

The clock at the bottom of the screen continued to count upward. The door at the top of the stairs continued to remain closed. Peters clicked a toggle, and the display slipped into fast-forward. People began to speed-walk as they went about their work.

Peters ran a hand across his scalp, dislodging his careful comb over. Turned to Munroe. "We're looking at having to dump nearly a full day's production. We're a small cannery, like I told you," Peters went on, "but we still load out six or seven rigs a day. So that'd be one hell of a lot of canned tomatoes." He turned away from the screen to face Munroe. Limp strands of hair hung down the side of his face and draped across his shoulder. The man looked ill. "But even worse … absolutely the worst … is having to tell daddy that we canned his baby girl. I really don't want to have to tell him that."

People continued to speed-walk while time flew by.

"So, we just keep watching that door," Peters said. "And see what happens." And to no one in particular: "Jeebus!"

"Is that the only way out?"

"There's a skylight." Peters paused. Then, "You didn't hear me say that."

"Well, here's another question while we wait. Of all your employees, who, in your estimation, might be the most likely to kill Ms. Edwards?"

"Oh God! Kill Brenda? No one. Everyone." He paused. Then, "There is Jensen, though. He's quiet. Keeps to himself.

Hardly ever talks, you know? Sometimes, I think he's on the spectrum. He's scary smart."

"A genius then."

"Isn't it the quiet types you gotta look out for?"

The two men returned to watch the image of people speed walking.

Then, "It's not that he thinks outside the box. It's like he designed the damned box in the first place. And then dimensioned it. If it really made sense to him, I think he could kill someone. But it would have to be logical. It would have to be the simplest solution."

"Like the hog."

"Don't say that.'

As the video showed four twenty-five, a man speed-walked into the picture. He had reached the base of the stairs before Peters could click the speed back to normal.

"That's Jensen. He must have spent all afternoon measuring the sluices. And Brenda is still waiting for him in his office."

"By now, she's either sleeping or incredibly pissed at having been kept waiting for so long," Munroe observed as Jensen reached the top and entered his office.

The recording continued to play in real-time. The door remained closed. Five minutes passed as the two men continued watching a closed door.

"Well, if she was pissed, that door would have opened by now."

"I have to agree with you," Munroe said. "Could they be secret lovers...?"

"Take me now Lord. Please!"

Peters went back to bumping the video in bursts of fast forward. The clock display inched toward five o'clock. And past five. At ten minutes after, the door finally opened. Jensen descended the stairs alone, a man without a care in the world. Peters fast-forwarded the video through another half hour, but the door never opened again.

Munroe looked at Peters. Peters returned the look. Blank.

Finally, Munroe spoke. "We need to talk to Jensen."

***

Peters started for the stairs, but Munroe stopped him.

"This could get violent. I'll go up first."

Munroe climbed the stairs quickly. He paused at the top, then pulled the door open.

The office was deserted. Wider than he had expected. A library table ran along the right-hand wall beneath the low, sloping roof. An old-fashioned skylight flooded the office with daylight. A raven alighting onto the roof caught his eye briefly. Behind him, tucked up against the front wall of the office, were a plotter and a blueprint machine.

In the center of the room was the engineer's desk, facing the door, sporting twin monitors. Against the back wall behind the desk was an old drawing board, a large sheet of paper taped to its surface with a drafting machine resting where a drawing had been started. Everything was exceptionally tidy. Compulsively so, Munroe thought.

A framed drawing hung on the wall to Munroe's left. A poster, a reproduction of an Escher drawing. M. C. Escher, idol of every draftsman.

"Optical illusion," he told himself. "Wonderfully done."

Peters came into the office, closing the door behind him. Munroe was distracted by two ravens disputing on the skylight. Peters looked at him quizzically.

"Ravens," Munroe said. "Camp followers of armies."

"I don't know what that means," Peters said.

"It's nothing. Jensen's not here, so let's have a seat. I can clear up a couple of details while we wait."

Peters took the engineer's chair, Munroe the guest chair in front of the desk.

Munroe pulled out his phone and punched in a number. "This will only take a minute," he told Peters. Then, into the phone, he requested prisoner transport and a crime scene investigation team.

"I can't imagine why Jensen would want to kill Brenda."

"I know," Munroe responded. "I can't either."

Peters looked at him blankly. Munroe returned the look. Said nothing. Birds skittered across the skylight; Peters turned his attention to his hands.

"Back in your office, I saw a photograph on your desk."

"My wife. Peggy. And our son Mark." Strands of hair still dangled limply down the side of his face. "Mark's going to be a sophomore at Chico State. Plays football—his coach thinks he might make senior varsity in the fall. Aaron Rodgers..."

"Yes, I know. You're having an affair with Janet Stokowski, aren't you?"

Peters came to a sudden halt. Full stop. Paused a moment, then slumped slightly in the chair. "Is it that obvious?"

"She gave it away when we were discussing Ms. Edwards," Munroe said.

Three birds lit upon the skylight, squabbling amongst themselves. Munroe looked up, studied them. Then looked back at Peters. Peters was sweating.

"She's on the roof, isn't she?" But it wasn't a question, really.

"She said she only wanted a thousand dollars. I honestly believed that would be the end of it." A tear ran down his right cheek.

"I got that impression."

"But how did..."

"You tried to distract me—you almost covered the monitor when it showed you coming down the stairs."

Peters slumped in the chair, fully deflated. Tears streamed down both cheeks. "What was I going to do? Brenda Edwards was a truly ugly woman."

Content warning: This story contains content about sexual assault.

THE LADY IN PINK

Joanna Vander Vlugt

I raised my sunglasses and peered through the passenger window of my Honda Civic at the Estelle Bakery and Pâtisserie sign. This was the right place. I checked my lipstick in the rearview mirror, grabbed my purse and stepped out.

At first, I thought the older woman under the archway was an apparition. Dressed in a pink paisley dress and pink boots, her face was partially hidden under a pink umbrella, but it wasn't raining. In fact, it was 84 degrees. Was she senior living Barbie? Her black-gloved hand raised a cigarette and smoke twined from under the umbrella. Senior living, smoking Barbie? Maybe not. Was this the woman I drove 750 miles to interview because she felt uncomfortable on Zoom and feared being hacked?

I stepped inside and smelled cinnamon, vanilla, and pastries. An employee wearing a gray apron, white shirt and chef's hat arranged macarons on a serving tray. Another employee with red hair and freckles took orders at the till.

"Welcome," the redhead said. "What can I get you?"

I admired the rows of pink and orange macarons, tuxedo bars, truffle cakes, and pear Danishes. I ordered an apple almond croissant and a latte. A family was just leaving, and I snagged their table.

A server brought my items.

"Thank you."

I bit into the croissant and groaned, tasting tart apple, cinnamon, and sugar. A whiff of smoke crept over my shoulders, and a black-gloved finger trailed on the marble near my mug.

The pink lady had followed me in.

Tall, shoulders back, her salt-and-pepper hair was swirled into a bun, like the icing on the truffle cakes. I guessed she was in her mid-fifties.

"Sorcha Lewis?" she asked in a voice reminiscent of Bette Davis.

This was her. The super fan of my true crime podcast. "Yes." I stood. "Mrs. Reynolds?"

"Nice to meet you," she said.

I grabbed a napkin, brushing crumbs from my cargo shorts, wishing I had upped my attire. Since lockdown, I dressed in a permanent state of casual.

"Please," I motioned to the chair across from me.

Mrs. Reynolds sat. She placed a dessert box decorated with sprigs of dry flowers in the center of the table beside the vase of white carnations. "For you. Welcome to Sacramento."

"That's very kind of you."

She smiled. "I listened to your podcast while knitting my son's cardigan. You're not what I imagined." She eyed my long, dark hair.

I hoped that was a compliment. I pushed my latte and croissant to the side, leaning in so I could hear her over the tourists occupying the table to our right. Mrs. Reynolds had emailed me in response to my information request about the unsolved disappearance of Brian Lancaster, the eighteen-year-old son of a senator and an all-round athlete. When he wasn't playing football, he enjoyed golf. Brian's golf bag, minus an expensive driver, and his Corvette were found at the Lune Golf and Country Club where he was last seen. Mrs. Reynolds said she had pertinent information. And that's how I found myself in Sacramento, renting an artist's bungalow for the weekend instead of on my houseboat in Lake Union. After this interview, I was going to Disneyland to see my boyfriend.

"Given Brian's disappearance happened thirty-something years ago, it's difficult to find people who still remember the incident," I said. "Did you know him?"

She averted her gaze, looking at the dessert box. I could have sworn her cheeks flushed.

"We both grew up here. He lived in Granite Bay, and I lived in Florin. We stirred in different circles."

I tugged my notepad from my purse. With my pencil poised, I flipped pages to my questions. I placed my phone on the table, my finger hovering over the record button. "Is it all right if I record our conversation?"

"Absolutely."

"When did you two meet?"

"In 1988, Sac may have been a Cowtown, but all the killer punk bands came through." Her eyes sparkled. "We had Birdcage Walk, and dollar movie night at the Birdcage Theatre. Joan Jett and the Blackhearts released their song *I Hate Myself for Loving You*, which had become my summer anthem. It was the end of the school year, and skaters were everywhere. My friends and I had come from the mall."

I leaned over my notepad as Mrs. Reynolds skated me back to 1988, old Sac.

***

"It's Joan Jett!" Bella shouted from the backseat of Andrea's Toyota, which they nicknamed the Mold-mobile. "Turn it up."

Andrea Walker, sometimes called A&W, cranked the volume on the car radio as she made a left onto Greenback Lane. Joan Jett was their hero. Andrea had dyed her brown hair black and wore spandex. She belted the chorus, no longer angry at her dad for refusing to unhitch his homemade covered trailer from the Toyota. Nothing screamed loser like that handyman special. She had been accepted into the dental hygienist program at Sac City College. Once she got a job, her first purchase would be a Triumph motorcycle.

Janey Collins sat in the passenger seat. Wearing shorts and a t-shirt, she tapped the beat on her bare legs. The window was rolled down, and the breeze tangled her blonde hair. She had one more year at Florin High, and she had no clue what she wanted to do with her life.

Bella Lise Taylor, or BLT, air guitared. She was going to study art at Berkeley, but today was her birthday. They had spent the Saturday morning doing a bakery crawl, then early afternoon shopping at Birdcage Walk. Stuffed with desserts and vibrating from too much sugar, they'd top off their celebrations by watching Poltergeist III. But first they needed to stop at the Lune Golf and Country Club so she could check her work schedule.

Andrea turned the volume down as she pulled into the golf course. "Hurry up. I'm illegally parked."

"No one will notice. Everyone's in the restaurant," Bella said, tugging on her shorts as she carefully lifted each leg so she didn't leave a layer of skin on the vinyl seat. "We might bump into Hottie Brian Lancaster. He's going to Harvard."

"I wouldn't be so gaga over him." Janey turned to face her. "He may come from money, but I've heard he sleeps around on his girlfriend and sometimes hits her."

"Douchebag," Andrea said, a lit cigarette in her mouth. She rolled down the driver's side window, blowing out smoke. "Do what you gotta do. We don't want to be late for the movie."

Bella popped out and ran towards the office, puffing up her hair. Her sister had spent four hours giving her a home perm so she could look like Julia Roberts. If only Brian would notice her.

Bella unlocked the front office door and stepped inside. She beelined to the wall calendar. Tomorrow, Sunday afternoon, was her next shift. The door opened again. She spun around.

Hottie Brian, with his chiseled jaw and wide shoulders, stood in the doorway. At first, he looked shocked to see her. A smile tugged at his lips, not quite making it. The door closed behind him.

"Hi," she said, standing straight.

"Bella, right?" he said, combing his fingers through his dark hair.

He knew her name. "Yes."

He placed his hands on his hips. "I'm looking for the golf pro."

"I don't know where he is."

He frowned.

Say something smart. "Did you get a hole-in-one?" she asked.

He eyed her breasts, then he reached behind and locked the door.

"What ... are you doing?" Bella asked.

He smugly smiled. "You've been eying me all year." He walked towards her, his golf bag slipping from his shoulder. He pushed her flat across the desk, knocking family photos on the floor.

A binder jabbed into Bella's spine. "Stop."

"I'm going to get that hole in one."

"Get off me!" She shrieked, hitting his chest.

He backhanded her.

Her cheek stung. "Get off," she screamed, squirming and kicking.

He grabbed her wrists and then smacked her again. "Shut up." He ripped open her summer blouse. "Look at them—"

then his eyes rolled to the back of his head, his knees buckled, and his body crumpled onto the floor.

Andrea loomed, clutching a golf club. "Are you alright?"

Bella scrambled upright, pulling her blouse closed. She brushed aside tears.

"Bella, are you alright?" Andrea repeated.

"He, he..."

"I know what he was trying to do. Jerk. I was wondering what was taking you so long. The door was locked, so I came in the back."

Janey marched into the office. "What the hell—" she saw Brian's body and the bloody gash on his head. She looked at Bella. "He tried to rape you, didn't he?"

Bella nodded, brushing aside tears.

"Is he dead?" Janey asked.

"Check his pulse," Andrea said.

"I don't want to touch the creep," Janey said.

"Well, I don't want to touch him, and Bella sure doesn't."

Janey stepped over his body and placed her hand near his nose. "He's breathing."

"We need to call the cops." Bella reached for the phone.

"No," Andrea and Janey said together.

"He tried—"

"You know who he is," Andrea said, pointing to the bloody golf club. "We can't leave him here."

"What are we going to do?" Bella couldn't look at him.

Janey dragged her hands over her face, reminding Bella of Edvard Munch's famous painting, The Scream. "It'll be your word against his."

"But Andrea's a witness," Bella countered.

"Middle-class girls seeing an opportunity to destroy the reputation of a popular high school quarterback," Andrea said. "We gotta get him and us outta here."

"And go where?" Janey asked.

"We'll leave him at Avery's Pond. Make it look like he passed out and hurt himself," Andrea said. "I'll bring the trailer around back."

***

My pencil lead snapped. I flicked it aside. "Have you told the police? The FBI?"

"The police knew that the last place Brian was seen alive was the golf course," Mrs. Reynolds said. "They questioned everyone, including Bella. I don't know the correct term, but they found blood and buttons on the floor."

Bella's buttons.

The redhead was now mopping. "Closing time, ladies," she called out.

Mrs. Reynolds stood. "Tomorrow, Sorcha. Ten a.m., same place. I will tell you more."

That night, I tossed and turned, replaying Mrs. Reynolds's conversation in my head. At three a.m., I propped myself up, turned on the pink Tiffany lamp and untangled the pink sheets from around my legs. I felt like spun cotton candy. Mrs. Reynolds would like this place. Why did she want to help now? The reason couldn't just be my podcast. Odd lady, yet she had hooked me up with this rental given it was the Farm-to-Fork Festival and the city was packed.

Later in the morning, when I arrived at the bakery, Mrs. Reynolds was already seated, again impeccably dressed in pink linen pants and matching shirt. She tapped a newspaper article. "Have you ever gone to The Farm-to-Fork Festival?"

"No," I said, sitting across from her. An almond croissant and latte waited.

"People come from around the world," she said. "A street festival of food, wine, music, capped by the Tower Bridge Dinner. My son provides the wine. You must go. Now, where did we leave off? Right, Andrea driving the Mold-mobile behind the office."

***

Andrea rubbed her forehead as she drove. She was out of smokes, and she had made a wrong turn. They were now on Madison Avenue and would be at Avery's Pond soon. She was certain she had pulled a muscle lugging Brian from the office into the trailer. Bella and Janey each held a leg, and Andrea had her arms slung under his upper body. She quickly tied his hands behind his back as Bella and Janey stood guard. This was kidnapping.

"Stop!" Janey shouted.

The car ahead was stopped at a red light. Andrea slammed on the brakes. Janey braced her hand against the glovebox, and Bella pushed back against the seat. Tires squealed; the trailer fishtailed.

Janey stared. "Earth to Andrea. If he dies, we're on the hook for murder. I'm sure Bella doesn't want to be painting impressionist prison portraits on her next birthday."

The traffic moved, and Andrea accelerated. "Nobody is going to jail. The jerk will think twice about raping another girl. Bella, you tell no one what happened. Understand?" Andrea eyed Bella in the rearview mirror.

Bella looked away at the passing vehicles. "We should have gone to the police."

Bang.

The Toyota swerved into the fast lane. A semi blared its horn.

"What's going on?" Janey shrieked.

Andrea steered the car back into the slow lane. "I don't know," she shouted.

Bella scrambled to look behind them. The trailer was attached but sparks sprayed from the back wheel. "You blew a tire. Hold on." Bella undid her seatbelt, rolled down the window and poked her head out, the wind whipping her face and hair.

"Bella! What are you doing?" Janey called out. "Get back in here."

Bella sat, rolling up the window. "The trailer has no left back wheel."

"Crap," Andrea said, struggling with the steering wheel. She reduced her speed.

A farm truck pulled up in the fast lane. The driver honked his horn and pointed for them to pull over.

"Crap!" Andrea slowed and stopped on the side of the road.

"Why are you stopping?" Janey exclaimed.

The truck parked behind them.

"I'll handle this." Andrea stepped out of the car and walked towards the farmer, who was eyeing the trailer.

Janey and Bella got out.

Andrea turned. "What are you doing?"

"We're also involved in this," Janey hissed.

"Say nothing," Andrea ordered. She turned towards the farmer, who looked to be in his mid-twenties. Wearing a black t-shirt and jeans, he could double as a cover model for a western romance novel.

"Your trailer's blown a wheel. It's riding on the axle hub. Do you have a spare?" he asked.

The girls looked at each other and said nothing.

"I'm taking that as a, no?"

Andrea shrugged. "We don't have a spare."

He looked at each of them. They were young, probably just graduating. The East Area Rapist was still out there, and he was the stranger on the side of the road. He held out a callused hand. "Marty Reynolds. I work at the vineyard."

The girls didn't move.

Marty placed his hand in his pocket. "You can't keep pulling this box on three wheels. You'll get into an accident."

Andrea was about to speak when a thump came from inside the trailer.

"What was that?" Marty asked.

Andrea cursed under her breath.

Another thump.

"What do you have in there?" Marty demanded.

"A pig," Janey said.

"Help!" More thumps from the trailer.

Marty's eyes grew wide. "There's a man in there."

The girls looked at each other.

"Open this. Now," Marty ordered.

Andrea ambled past him. She inserted the key into the lock and lifted the cover.

Amongst paint cans and rollers, a man squirmed and kicked from under a tarp. Marty flung it back. Brian Lancaster, sweating and bloody, panted. Marty held his hair back from his face. "Holy crap."

"You gotta help me, man!" Brian pleaded.

"What the hell are you doing with him?" Marty asked Andrea.

"They kidnapped me," Brian shouted, flopping around like a sea lion. "Get me out!"

"He—"

"Bella," Andrea warned, cutting her off.

"No. She has something to say," Marty said. "He what, Bella? That's your name?"

"Yes," Bella said.

"What did he do?" Marty asked.

"Nothing!" Brian shouted.

"You shut up," Marty said. He stepped toward her, seeing her bruised and swollen cheek. "Did he hit you?"

Bella's lip trembled.

"Worse. He tried to rape her," Janey blurted.

"They're lying." Brian kicked the trailer.

"If we hadn't walked in, Douchebag would have succeeded," Andrea said.

Marty looked again at Bella.

Her blouse was pinned with safety pins where buttons were missing. She looked at the ground.

"Is this true?" he asked.

"Yes," she said. "Thank God Andrea walked in."

The color drained from Marty's face. His eyes narrowed as he looked at Brian. "You raped her."

"She wanted it."

Marty stepped up to the trailer and dropped the cover, muffling Brian's shouts. "Why'd I stop?" Marty muttered, pacing. "Why'd I stop? Be a good Samaritan. Prevent an accident. Do something nice." He turned to Andrea. "He has a bloody head. What'd ya hit him with?"

"His driver. It's in the back seat."

"You brought it with you?" Marty rubbed his face. "What did you hope to do?"

"Make it look like he got drunk and hit his head at Avery's Pond." Andrea paused. "And if that didn't work, do what they do in the movies: give him cement sneakers and drop him in the lake."

Janey and Bella swung around, staring at Andrea.

"You didn't tell us that," Janey said.

"First, he's conscious," Marty said. "Second, you know how to mix concrete? Or were you going to have Brian Lancaster stand there while a concrete truck backed up and poured concrete on his shoes, and then drag him because you're not strong enough to pick him up, to the lake and toss him in and hope no one notices!"

"You're a big, strong guy; maybe you'd do it," Andrea said.

Marty glared. "Not a chance."

"We didn't plan this." Andrea raised her voice. "It's Bella's birthday. We were doing a bakery crawl, a little shopping and were going to a movie. Brian needs to be held accountable."

Marty pointed at the trailer. "Not by killing him! You don't think the senator, the sheriffs, and the FBI won't be looking for him?" He braced his hands against the trailer and cursed. He straightened and pinched the inner corners of his eyes. "This is a wooden box on wheels, right?"

"Yes," Andrea nodded. "My dad made it. He paints houses."

"Lock it," Brian ordered.

Andrea did so. Brian screamed louder.

"You're going to unhitch the trailer. Then all of us" —he looked at the girls— "are wheeling the trailer over to my truck, and all of us are lifting it onto the flatbed. I'll strap it down."

"You're taking him?" Andrea said.

"Unless you want to explain to your dad why there's blood in his trailer." Marty walked backwards to his truck.

"We'll do it," Bella said. She looked at Andrea. "You heard him unhitch the trailer." Bella looked back at Marty. "Where are you taking him?"

"Like your friend said, Avery's Pond."

***

I leaned back in my chair. "What did Marty do to Brian?"

Mrs. Reynolds focused on her mug, her thumbs circling.

"Mrs. Reynolds?"

"Sorcha, I'm tired. Tomorrow."

"Same time, same place," I said reluctantly.

At the artist's bungalow, I tossed back a scotch, thinking of our conversation. I tapped the glass against the counter and stared at a painting of Avery's Pond. The sky was reflected in blues and pinks, and the artist had captured the reflection of oak trees. I stepped closer to the painting, looking for the artist's signature. What was that, by a blackberry bush? Was that ... a headstone? Written on it were the initials BLT. I flipped the pages of my notes and tapped the initials on the page. Bella's nickname. What happened to these girls? What happened to Marty? Had they murdered Brian? And which one of the girls was Mrs. Reynolds?

The next morning, while sitting at our table, Mrs. Reynolds lifted her cup with a trembling hand. She looked tired. I wanted to press on but felt guilty seeing her fatigue. "Mrs. Reynolds, we don't have to do an interview today."

"No," she said, her Bette Davis voice rougher. "It's time to get this out in the open. We left off with Andrea unhitching the trailer."

***

Andrea tapped her thumb on the steering wheel as they drove away from Marty's farm truck. "How am I going to explain the missing trailer to my dad?"

"Tell him someone stole it," Janey said, adjusting her seatbelt.

Andrea groaned and turned off the radio.

"Does your dad golf?" Janey asked. "We still have the golf club. Clean it up and give it to him for Father's Day."

"Janey, that makes no sense," Andrea said.

"Maybe we should go to Avery's Pond," Bella said quietly.

Janey turned, the seatbelt tight across her body. "And do what? Cheer like the Sac State Cheerleaders? Marty's taking care of Brian."

"We should have left him in the office," Bella continued. "Maybe he wouldn't say anything."

Janey's eyes flared. "People with money protect people with money. No one would believe us."

"Janey, chill," Andrea said. She looked at Bella in the rear-view mirror. "Bella, do you want to go to Avery's Pond?"

Bella nodded.

Andrea's foot hit the brake.

Janey braced her hand against the dash as she was pressed against the door. "This ... is ... so ... wrong."

With both hands gripping the steering wheel, Andrea made a left and floored it. "Marty shouldn't be hard to find."

They pulled into the parking lot and saw his farm truck. Andrea parked beside it. The trailer was still on the flatbed. There were a few cars, but they couldn't see Marty or Brian. They got out.

"The trail," Andrea pointed, walking uphill.

Bella and Janey caught up to her. They ran past evergreen shrubs and came to three forks.

"This way to the pond," Andrea said, taking the right trail. They stepped over a fallen tree. A blackberry vine scratched Bella's legs.

A gunshot.

Four deer leapt across the trail ahead of them, disappearing into the underbrush.

"I'm out of here." Janey ran the way they had come.

Andrea and Bella followed. Bella tripped on a branch and landed with an oomph, hitting her chest. On the ground, just out of her reach, a handgun landed. She scrambled to her knees and picked it up.

"Bella." Marty ran behind her. Blood stained his t-shirt, and his right eye was swollen shut. "Hand it over," he said, out-of-breath.

Bella hesitated.

"C'mon," Marty said. "It's my gun. Brian's coming. He's dangerous."

She stepped towards him.

A crash and snap of branches, Brian burst from the trees. His nose was bloody, and he had dirt on his face and moss in his hair. He lunged.

Bella squeezed the trigger.

His body spasmed and dropped.

"No!" Marty shouted.

Andrea and Janey ran up to Bella and stared. Brian Lancaster, his eyes glazed, blood saturating his white golf shirt, lay dead.

Andrea looked from Bella to Marty and back to Bella.

"I killed him," Bella cried.

"You acted in self-defense," Andrea corrected, her voice shaky.

Bella motioned with the gun. "Someone take it. Take it."

"Stay calm." Marty's arm brushed against her. "I've got it." He placed his callused hands over hers.

Bella let go.

"That's good," he said, looking her in the eye. "You're going to be okay, Bella, understand?"

Janey, with fear in her eyes, pointed at Brian's body. "Now what?"

Marty flicked the safety catch and tucked the gun into the waist of his pants. "The three of you are getting the hell out of here." He wiped blood and sweat from his face with his shirt. "I'll get rid of..." He nodded at Brian's body. "Him. Andrea, I'm going to need that tarp." He pointed at them. "You can't say a damn thing, understood? Because if anyone talks, we implicate each other. Got it?"

They nodded.

"I didn't hear you?" Marty pressed.

"Got it," they said.

***

I stopped writing. Mrs. Reynolds took a tissue from her purse and dabbed the corners of her eyes. I wanted to reach out and squeeze her hand. Which girl are you?

She snapped the catch on her purse. Her lips quivered. "I must go." She looked outside. "My son gave me two tickets to the Tower Bridge Dinner tomorrow." Her hand trembled as she slid a ticket towards me. "We'll meet on the bridge at the Sacramento sign. I'll finish my story."

"I'll be there."

She nodded, hesitated, and then, leaning on her umbrella, made her way out of the bakery. Mrs. Reynolds was no longer the tall, resilient woman I met two days ago. I should have offered to walk with her.

The redhead wiped down the table.

"She's going to be okay, right? Or should I go after her?" I asked.

"Mrs. Reynolds is the most resourceful woman I know. Some people say she's a bit loopy," the cashier made circles with her finger, "but I love her. Have you met her son?"

"No."

"He'll be at the Tower Bridge Dinner. John Reynolds."

The next evening, with the sun shining, the Tower Bridge looked more a bright yellow than gold. Dressed in a blue sleeveless dress I had purchased that afternoon, along with heels that were killing my feet, I strolled from the laughter and live jazz towards the large letters stretching across the bridge, spelling SACRAMENTO. Oh, Mrs. Reynolds. I hope you're okay. I tapped the "M" with my fist. Two rows of tables stretched across the length of the bridge. Dinner was about to be served to eight hundred guests. I headed to Table 25, pulled out my chair and sat. Vases of sunflowers made festive centerpieces. I placed the cloth napkin on my lap, not feeling festive at all. I craned my neck, searching for an elegantly dressed lady in pink.

As a band played, I ate an amazing Jamaican-styled roasted duck, a dish with smoked peaches and sunflowers, fresh tuna marinated in coconut cream, and lost track of the courses. I made polite conversation with the couple on my right while glancing at the empty chair across from me.

After dessert, I squeezed between people laughing, clinking wine glasses, and taking selfies. I again stood at the letter "M."

"Sorcha Lewis?"

I turned. An attractive man stood, dressed in a suit and holding a glass of white. His sunglasses hid his eyes.

"Yes."

"John Reynolds of Reynolds Vines. Mrs. Reynolds, or Mom, wanted to pass on her regrets. She won't be joining you."

"Is she alright?"

"Now, yes. She gave my wife and me a scare. She didn't come home for dinner last night."

"Where was she?" I asked.

"We found her at eight o'clock way over in Citrus Heights. She could have been hit by a car, abducted. She said she wanted to go to Avery's Pond. I understand you've been interviewing her."

"Yes, for my true crime podcast. We were discussing the disappearance of Brian Lancaster."

John Reynolds sipped his wine and looked over the Sacramento River.

"Will I be able to see Mrs. Reynolds again?" I asked.

"No."

Not a maybe, or I'll check with Mom, but a definite no. I could still put together an interesting episode, and the unsolved mystery of Brian would be intriguing, but I wanted to know what happened to his body, Marty Reynolds and especially the girls. "I was hoping Mrs. Reynolds could fill in a few outstanding details."

John stepped closer. "Mom has Early-Onset Alzheimer's. She has good days and bad days. Sometimes, she forgets she tells people things." He whipped off his sunglasses. "Why are you digging this up?"

I was unnerved by his hostility. "I-I didn't know. She reached out to me."

John cursed. "I'll tell you what I know on one condition."

"And what's that?"

"Leave my mom's name and my name out of your podcast."

"I can do that. So, what happened to Andrea, Janey and Bella?"

"They remained friends." He sipped his wine. "Janey became a wealthy litigation lawyer. She died ten years ago from cancer. Andrea became a dental hygienist, bought her Triumph, but she died in her mid-twenties in a motorcycle accident."

"That's horrible. And Bella?"

John looked over the Sacramento River and the boats moored below. Back went on his sunglasses. "Bella went to Berkeley and became an artist. She worked at Reynolds Vines one summer when Marty took it over. They got married before he went overseas to fight in the Gulf War. He was killed in action." He swirled his wine. "I never got to meet my father, but my mom told me a lot about him, and ... what happened. She recently said someone needed to know before she lost her mind. I guess you're that someone."

I paused, my wine glass at my lips. "Your mom, Mrs. Reynolds..."

"Is Bella."

I felt relief and excitement. I had been interviewing Bella, BLT. She and Marty had fallen in love, and this dashing man was their son.

"She regrets killing him. Her innocence died that day. Brian was a rapist, and like my dad, I would have beaten the crap out of him too. Mom always says I have a son; the Lancasters never knew what happened to theirs."

"What did Marty—your dad—do with the body?"

John raised his glass. "Check Mom's painting in the bungalow you're staying at." He smiled. "That was her place before she moved in with me and my wife."

THE SACRAMENTO TRUCK FARM

Elaine Faber

Jean Ann opened her eyes and turned her head away from the sunlight pouring through her bedroom window. She squealed and scrunched her shoulders. "It's my birthday! Now that I'm thirteen years old, I can solve crimes just like Nancy Drew."

Mom's voice called from the kitchen, "Jean Ann. Breakfast is almost ready!"

"February 16th, 1928! Isn't it the greatest-sounding date?" Jean Ann said. "I wonder what Mom bought me for my birthday?" She climbed out of bed, dressed hurriedly in coveralls and a long-sleeved shirt and ran a brush through her hair. Today was her day to help at the fruit stand. She'd have to braid her hair later. It wouldn't do to have her hair down while carrying the customers' crates of strawberries, lettuce, and spinach to their cars.

Mama's fruit stand was known all over the Sacramento Valley for fresh fruit and vegetables, and Saturday was the busiest day of the week. But since today was her birthday, shouldn't they close the fruit stand and take a nice trip to the brand-new zoo that just opened in Sacramento last year? Jean Ann reached for her favorite book on the nightstand. Nancy Drew and The Secret of the Old Clock. She grabbed her worn notebook, where she posted her own clues and lists of suspects, and carried the two books downstairs. Pa was already at the breakfast table reading the local newspaper.

"What's going on today, dear," Mama scooped scrambled eggs and bacon onto Pa's plate.

"People are making money hand over fist in the stock market, Millicent. We should talk to someone about investing our little nest egg in the stock market."

Mama poured milk into the cat's bowl, "You heard what Pastor said in church last week about gambling! If I've told you once, I've told you a thousand times that the stock market is just another form of gambling! We should use our nest egg to upgrade the fruit stand. At least buy me a heater. It gets so cold down there this time of year."

Pa scowled and shook the paper. "Yes, dear." He read for a moment and said, "Listen to this. The Winter Olympics are in St. Moritz, Switzerland, this year. The USA team has already taken a few medals with four days to go." He flipped the pages to the Farm and Agriculture section. He was likely checking the price of lettuce, the vegetable they'd be harvesting over the next few months.

"Pa. Did you remember today is my birthday?" Jean Ann set her fork on the table and scooted her notebook closer to her plate. "When can we go to the Sacramento Zoo? Mama said..."

"No, honey, not today. Saturday is the fruit stand's busiest day. You know, after we send the main crop to market, we always sell what's left at a discount to our neighbors on Saturday morning."

"Yes, Pa." Jean Ann's hair swung across her face as she lowered her head. It seemed that Pa hadn't remembered her birthday after all. Maybe he didn't even buy her a present.

"Oh, Millicent," Pa said. "Don't we have a little something for Jean Ann's birthday?"

"That's right. I think there's a surprise in the living room."

Jean Ann raced to the living room and stood with her mouth open and hands clasped at the sight of a tall Atwater

Kent radio with beautifully carved legs, gold grill cloth, and delightful dials. "Oh my!" Pa and Mama followed her into the living room, and Pa twisted the dials until the radio hummed, and he located a music station. "They have news, and stories, as well as music. Tonight, we can sit in the living room and listen to all sorts of programs."

"But now, we need to open the fruit stand," Mama said. "Someone has to make some money to pay for our new playthings."

Jean Ann ran her hand over the beautiful, rich-colored walnut radio and sighed. How she wished she could sit and listen to the music now. What a lovely birthday surprise.

Within the hour, Jean Ann and Mama were at the fruit stand with the large panels on the front facing the street opened. Jean Ann sorted through the crates of yesterday's fruit and vegetables and removed any that looked slightly wrinkled or bruised. Before long, their neighbors began to arrive and Mama rang up the sales. No matter the size of the order, Jean Ann always carried their purchases to the car. Mama said it was an unexpected service they owed the customer that brought them back again and again. Jean Ann doubted it made much difference, but sometimes a rich tourist would give her a quarter as a tip, so she was always on hand to volunteer, particularly if they drove fancy cars like a Chrysler Imperial or town car.

When there were no customers, Jean Ann would ply Mama with details from the storylines of her Nancy Drew books. She liked to read from her notebook about her own mystery cases, like who stole the long johns off the clothesline last summer or who ate the last piece of pumpkin pie last week.

Just before lunchtime, Jean Ann ran back to the house to retrieve her notebook she left on the kitchen table. She couldn't resist sneaking a peek into the living room to admire the new radio. It wouldn't hurt to turn it on for just a minute, would it?

She turned the dial and jumped back when the volume loudly came on with a local news report. The Elk Grove Security Bank and Trust was just robbed by two roughly-dressed men in greasy mechanics coveralls, wearing masks and brandishing revolvers. They held the manager, a board member, the teller, and three customers at gunpoint. They emptied the registers, made the manager open the vault, and got away with $8,200! A third bandit awaited them outside in a getaway vehicle. Another accomplice jumped into the getaway car and they escaped out of town without police pursuit. Another bank in a nearby town had been robbed of $10,000 just days before by similar bandits. Oh my!

Jean Ann's heart pounded. A real live crime! If she could solve this mystery, she would be a local hero. Maybe even get her picture in the Sacramento Bee. But, stuck on a truck farm, there was no way to bring her exceptional sleuthing powers to the forefront and capture the ruffians. She grabbed her notebook, made some hasty notes about the newscast, and ran back to the fruit stand to tell her mother about the robbery. She bragged about how she would bring the brigands to justice if she was ever lucky enough to confront them.

"Now Jean Ann, don't be such a silly goose. You and your gumshoe stories! I don't have time to listen to your tall tales." She turned away and began to dust the shelves where she stacked jars of strawberry jam and boysenberry jelly she sold on consignment for an elderly neighbor.

Jean Ann flumped onto a stool with her arms crossed. She was every bit as clever as Nancy Drew. There was no reason for Mama to belittle her abilities in solving mysteries or bringing ruffians to justice.

A large town car pulled to a stop in front of the fruit stand, and four men in greasy coveralls stepped out and wandered through the fruit stand picking up apples and cold drinks from the cooler. One man examined the jams and jellies and brought a jar of boysenberry jelly to the counter.

Jean Ann's eyes nearly popped out of her head. As sure as God made little green apples, it had to be the bank robbers! Four men, dressed in greasy clothes, just like the robbers, driving a Chrysler Imperial, just like the radio said. Well, sort of like the radio said… Wouldn't you expect that bank robbers could drive an expensive car like a Chrysler Imperial, considering all the money they stole? Now, how was she going to capture four armed men with a sweet tooth for apples and jelly?

Like a bolt from the blue, an ingenious idea came into her cunning detective brain. If she let the air out of their tires, she could run back to the house and call the authorities. They could raid the fruit stand and capture the miscreants before they had time to fix the tire and escape.

It never entered her head how four desperados would react when they discovered her scheme or the danger to herself and her mother, should the police's arrival result in a shoot-out. Jean Ann sneaked around the far side of the town car. While the men were munching on their apples and drinking their Nehi Cola, she unscrewed the cap on the driver's side rear tire air valve, inserted a bobby pin into the valve and applied pressure. The air hissed out of the inner tube and the tire flattened toward the ground. She hurried to the front tire and repeated the procedure. Within minutes, the car listed south.

Jean Ann covered her mouth to keep from laughing out loud, envisioned her picture in the local paper, hailed as a hero for bringing about the capture of the grubby villains and raced toward the house to alert the vice squad of their need to come and take charge of the scoundrels. Having placed her call and assured that the constabulary was hot on their trail, she hurried back to the fruit stand to await the felons' capture.

She was not surprised to find the men quite agitated, having discovered the plight of their vehicle with two flat tires. "Now, who on earth would do such a thing," Mama asked? "I'm so terribly sorry. I can't imagine..." She turned toward Jean Ann, sitting with her hand over her mouth, holding back her snickers. "Jean Ann! Come here this instant. What do you know about this ... this ... dreadful attack on Governor Young's new car?" She jerked her finger toward the lopsided 1928 Chrysler Imperial town car.

Jean Ann pulled her hand away from her mouth, and her snickers ceased. Her mouth dropped open, and her eyes fluttered in disbelief. "The governor's car? Aren't these the men who robbed the Elk Grove bank this morning?" She glanced down at her notebook and read her neatly numbered list, one through three, as to how and why she had come to believe they were the bank robbers. Hadn't the radio said four men, roughly dressed, driving a big car ... and ...

"Oh, crud muffins. What have I done?" Now, to make matters worse, not only were the four men righteously furious about the flat tires on the governor's car, but the police were on their way, expecting to arrest dangerous criminals. She cringed, hearing sirens in the distance, growing louder. "I called the police, Mama. That's them, coming now." After what she had done, she'd probably be grounded until 1935!

Much to her surprise, Mama began to laugh. The men chuckled and then doubled over, laughing until tears flowed down their cheeks. "Oh, Jean Ann."

Of course, the police screeched to a stop, guns drawn, scowls pasted on their stern faces. The four men dutifully raised their hands and stood quite still while Mama wiped tears off her face and explained the situation. Once they read

Governor C.C. Young's name on the car's registration papers and noticed his special license plate, they lowered their guns, gave Jean Ann a good scolding, and got back in their squad cars.

The four Sacramento Capitol White House garage mechanics retrieved a hand pump from the trunk, pumped up the tires, handed their Nehi Cola bottles to Mama to return for its three-cent deposit, and drove away.

"Well, Jean Ann, I hope you've learned your lesson today. It's best to leave solving crimes to storybook writers and the Sacramento Police Department."

Jean Ann hung her head. "Yes, Mama. And, if I live to be a hundred, February 16, 1928, is one birthday I'll never forget."

FORK AND KNIFE

Dänna Wilberg

"Isn't it grand?" Ruby Fredericks traced the gilt lettering with a stiletto-shaped fingernail and opened the leather-bound menu.

"You'd think at these prices, the staff would wipe these things off," griped her husband. John spread the pages wider and pointed to the red blotches defacing the description under the Fork and Knife section.

"Look at this place," Ruby said with a sweeping hand, "all the work it took to re-open. It's gorgeous and so—classy."

John's focus remained on the stains. "Too dark to be tomato sauce," he mumbled.

"Here." Ruby moved closer to her husband, offering her menu and a salacious smile. "Let's look together." Her shoulder pressed his. "What do you have a taste for?"

"Oh, baby, you know what I like," he replied, imitating the bassy "Big Bopper."

Ruby rolled her eyes and returned to the selections. "This fresh-caught salmon with brown butter and citrus sauce sounds divine."

"I'm leaning towards steak," he said, his finger following the words as he read, "Mosher's Simangus beef provides the perfect taste and tenderness." He nibbled her ear. "Just like you, my darling."

Ruby pulled away and fluffed her thick, chestnut-colored hair. "Go ahead—clog your arteries—see if I care."

"Seriously? You're going to start?"

"Let's just order. I don't want to miss my shows."

"Why did you insist we come here tonight if you're in such a hurry?" John's raised brow collapsed into a scowl. "You wanted to see Lover Boy, is that it? Is that why we're here?"

"It's Ésquisito's grand reopening—it has nothing to do with Phil. I thought you'd want to show your support. After all, you sold Giovanni the property in the first place."

"Silly me, what was I thinking?" He brought her hand to his lips and stopped. "You broke a nail—"

"Is it that noticeable?" She glanced at the break. "I had a new girl."

John nodded. "That explains it." He returned her hand to her lap. His eyes searched the room. "Where's our waiter? I need a drink."

***

Chef-owner Giovanni Gaballo ripped off his apron and stomped around the kitchen, flailing his arms. "How could he do this to me?"

Stephanie Bell followed in his wake. The rest of the staff focused on their work, pretending to ignore the outburst.

"I thought he'd at least be here for the opening," she said.

"I've called him fifty times; he's not picking up, and his voicemail is full."

"I can fill in—"

"You're one of the best demi chefs I've ever worked with, but you're not—"

"Phil?" Stephanie's voice rose a notch. "How do you know I'm not just as good as Phil or better unless you give me a chance?"

***

Detective Dan Calian navigated the sterile hallway of the County Morgue to the last door on the left. He slipped into the room with authority. "How long?" He lifted the sheet and peeked at the corpse.

Coroner Benjamin Chow cocked his head. "Seventy-two hours, give or take. I haven't finished my tests."

"What do we know?"

"Severe penetration wounds to the abdomen. He bled out."

Dan leaned closer to the body, focusing on the dead man's arm. "Interesting scars."

"Burns. They're faded. Most likely eight to ten years old. From the pattern, I'd say they're grease burns. My granddaughter went to culinary school—she was always burning herself. She opted out, thank god—became a teacher."

"Have you sent his clothing to forensics yet?"

Ben produced a sealed clear bag with blood-soaked clothing. The detective examined the contents through the plastic and noticed a few short white hairs that didn't appear to be from a human. He handed the bag back to Ben. "What about the hairs?"

"Working on it."

"Let me know what you find."

"Will do." Ben resumed his examination.

Dan reversed his steps down the hallway, his head spinning. *What a way to start the day.*

***

Dan had his work cut out for him. The neighbor who dialed 911 had identified the body as Phillip Maltese.

After a little digging, Dan learned the victim was from Chicago and had come to California to attend CASA, a culinary school in the Bay Area, fifteen years ago. After graduating, he went back to Chicago, worked his way up to sous chef at Three Forks, was fired for screwing the owner's married daughter, and fled to Sacramento. Dan was able to contact Phil's aunt in Chicago, who claimed the owner's daughter was to blame for the affair. "Women were always chasing him—such a looker."

***

The next day, Dan paid Ésquisito a visit. Giovanni sat slumped in a chair, one arm dangling over the back. Stephanie stood with her arms folded across her chest. Neither one showed any grief.

"How long did Phil work here?"

Giovanni flipped an open palm at the detective. "He helped me open the place eight years ago."

"Was he a partner?"

"Not on paper. He didn't have the money to invest. I paid him well; he worked his tail off, and we got along."

Dan turned to Stephanie. "How long have you worked here?"

"About six years. Covid shut us down in March of 2020."

Giovanni piped in. "Yeah, then we got hit hard when protests in Sacramento became destructive in May and again in August. It's taken this long to rebuild." He swiped his hand across his face and shook his head. "We just reopened for chrissake."

"Did Phil have enemies?"

Giovanni grunted. "Who doesn't in this business?"

Stephanie shrugged. "Phil was as arrogant as they come."

Dan learned that Stephanie had stepped in for Phil when he didn't show up for work the night of the grand reopening. No longer a station chef, she was headed for the big time. Her vibe made Dan pay close attention.

"What was your relationship with Mr. Maltese?" He watched her chin tilt upward and her fingers dance across her clavicle.

"We were co-workers," she said.

"Did you see each other outside of work?"

Stephanie shot a quick glance toward her boss, then met Dan's suspicions dead on. "What are you insinuating?"

"If you'd rather come down to the station to answer my questions, I can certainly understand."

Giovanni rose, his complacent demeanor morphing into anger. "Either arrest us—or get the hell out of my restaurant—I've got fifty people coming for an anniversary celebration tonight—I don't have time for this crap. And neither does she."

Dan sensed there was more to tell but now wasn't the time. He dipped two fingers in his shirt pocket and withdrew a couple of business cards. "If you think of anything, call me."

Back in his car, he ran Giovanni and Stephanie's plates. The two cars parked side-by-side seemed to symbolize their relationship. He was the shiny black Cadillac SUV, she was the sun-bleached-blue Ford Focus.

***

Ruby Fredericks adjusted the straps on the sapphire evening dress she had bought for the Farm-to-Fork gala being held on the Tower Bridge in September. John's status in the community as one of the top commercial investment brokers in California assured them an invite every year. *Too bad Phil won't be preparing one of his scrumptious dishes.* She sighed. *I miss him already.*

She hung the dress in the walk-in closet and opened the top drawer of the chest in the middle of the room. She slipped her hand beneath the velvet lining and came away with a photo of her and Phil in a compromising position. Had she known he had hidden cameras in his love nest, she would've thought better of her indiscretion. *What a stupid thing to do.* She glanced at her newly mended fingernail, stuffed the photo back into its hiding place, and slammed the drawer.

***

John Fredericks sipped his coffee while he studied the MLS listing of available properties. Midtown homes had flooded the market earlier that year after the area was rezoned to allow small businesses to hob-nob with homeowners. John flipped the page. He was more interested in acreage and commercial properties. One ad caught his eye. Vivé, a small French restaurant, was on the market. He had taken Ruby there on one of their first dates. She loved dining alfresco. He loved showing her off. After they married, she helped him out, greeting clients and sealing deals with her alluring charm. These thoughts led to memories of when he'd sold what was to become Ésquisito to Giovanni Gaballo. He remembered the day like it was yesterday...

"We want to turn the property into a restaurant. The building has good bones, a large area for seating, and space for a gourmet kitchen."

Gaballo's partner, Phil, agreed. "The building is unique, like our cuisine."

John remembered watching Ruby transform that day from doting wife to vixen, and the thought of losing her to a sous chef with a pretty face turned his stomach. But money talks ... Ironically, they closed the deal with a bottle of Vivé's champagne.

John wasn't surprised when the building's twelve-foot glass windows were smashed and all of their hard work was demolished during the protests in 2020. The insurance company was slow paying for damages. Specialty equipment was difficult to replace due to a decline in resources during Covid. Marble statues imported from Italy were smashed, and the ornate gold fixtures Giovanni had hand-picked during visits to his homeland were ripped from the walls and stolen. The total damages came in at 4.2 million dollars. Giovanni's insurance only covered three. For a solid year he limped along, focused on rebuilding. Then another Covid shutdown got the best of him, and he was forced to close his doors. Phil collected unemployment and had a lot of time on his hands. He managed to keep those hands busy. The thought made John's blood pressure soar. Stress made him hungry.

He pulled a chub of salami from the fridge and sliced it with the knife Giovanni had gifted him the day they closed the deal on Ésquisito. Phil's words rang in his head. "Here's to a slice of life." Suddenly, he lost his appetite.

***

Dan popped a TV dinner in the microwave, set the timer, and turned on Netflix. He spread Phil's crime scene photos on his concrete coffee table and set up a wooden tray. He went to the fridge, opened one of the lagers he'd purchased at Fieldworks Tap Room last week, and collected his grub. With every bite of his Salisbury steak and instant mashed potatoes, he wondered who had a motive for killing the high-profile sous chef?

According to Google and the photos he printed from the internet, Phil was a celebrity, winning several awards for Ésquisito, including a Michelin star, three years after he came to work for Giovanni. Dan studied photos of the young sous chef standing beside Giovanni, along with the likes of Kevin Costner, John Travolta, Tom Cruise, Penelope Cruz, Arnold Schwarzenegger, and Taylor Swift. Stephanie appeared in a few photos, along with beautiful models and several couples Dan didn't recognize. *One of these photos holds a clue.* Or so he hoped.

***

When Stephanie wasn't running her butt off, more so now that she was picking up the slack for Phil at Ésquisito, she was doing some profound worrying. She worried about neglecting her mother, who she hadn't talked to in over two weeks. She worried about throwing food at her cat on the way out the door every morning and feeling too tired to cuddle with her at night when she got home. Were the tufts of cat hair littering the carpet an indication that her stress was contagious? She worried she wouldn't measure up to Phil, and most of all, she worried the detective would find out about their fling. She dwelled on the last time they had sex, the harsh words after and how the proverbial knives had come out in more ways than one. *He shouldn't have said that to me.*

The knock on the door startled her. She peeked through the peep-hole. *Him.* She held her breath. Another knock, louder this time. She chewed her thumbnail to steady her nerves. "Just a minute," she called. She undid the chain lock and twisted the deadbolt. "Kind of early for a social visit."

Dan glanced at his watch. "I wanted to catch you between shifts."

"I'm not sure there is such a thing anymore," she said, opening the door. "Ever hear team work makes the dream work?"

"How's that going for you?" He stepped inside, shutting the door behind him.

"You certainly didn't come here to act as my career coach. What can I do for you, Detective?"

"I had a long chat with Phil Maltese's neighbors—showed them a few photos I snagged from the internet. One of them claimed they saw you two nights before Phil's body was discovered."

"Yes. I stopped by his apartment to confirm he was going to be at the re-opening."

"And why wouldn't he be? He worked there."

Stephanie's gaze dropped to her bare feet. "Yes," she said and lifted her head. "He did, but he wasn't always dependable."

"And the owner put up with that?"

"Let me rephrase. Phil had a way of keeping everyone in suspense."

"Enlighten me."

"I'm sure Giovanni will confirm. Phil tended to let his personal life override his commitments. He was notorious for not answering his phone or his texts."

"What about your texts? Did he answer yours?"

"What are you implying?"

"It's my job to part every hair."

Stephanie's thumbnail slid between her teeth. "We were colleagues—of course we talked."

"Nothing more?"

Her face warmed. She imagined her cheeks were blossoming red, contradicting her next answer. "We were colleagues, nothing more."

The detective turned for the door, sniffing the air. "You have a cat?"

"Yes. Britches. Why?"

"What color?"

"She's a calico."

"Phil didn't have a cat, did he?"

"Not that I was aware of..."

"Thank you for your time, Ms. Bell." Dan let himself out.

***

Giovanni rested his head in his palm. The whirring sound of the refrigerator motor reminded him he needed to call the service company. *More bills.* He rubbed his eyes, gritty from lack of sleep.

The calamity of reopening his restaurant robbed him of his daily winks, along with breaking Stephanie in as sous chef to oversee the menu and specialty dishes and hiring someone to take her place as demi chef to orchestrate each station.

Stephanie had managed to do both jobs surprisingly well with very little help from the rest of the staff, and he wondered if he shouldn't continue the status quo. *Throw a few more bucks her way, praise her publicly ... that's what she wanted, wasn't it? To be in the limelight? Like Phil?* He'd do anything to make her happy.

Phil. He pictured the man's handsome face. His stomach churned. He felt sick. *Why did you betray me?*

***

Later that afternoon, Dan sat at his desk pouring over magazine articles and newspaper clippings dating back to the year Phil returned to Sacramento. He cross-checked names and faces with those he found from Phil's past in Chicago. The only data that contained any dirt was from a gossip columnist in the Chicago Tribune. The writer claimed Three Forks' "golden boy" may have blackened the restaurant's eye in more ways than one by stepping out with the owner's married daughter and leaving his post as one of the best sous chefs since Gordon Ramsey.

Dan had worked on many cases dealing with infidelity; it was a common motive for murder, and usually, facts about the cheating participants were easily obtained. So far, all he had was one possible lie.

When five o'clock came around, he hit the road. Twenty minutes later, he bellied up to the bar at Tank House BBQ and ordered a beer.

Trina, the barmaid, laid down a napkin and flashed a Hollywood smile. "What brings you this way, Calian?"

He had picked up Trina years ago in a drug bust. She had been a minor at the time and was being trafficked by her uncle. He went to prison; she landed in foster care until she turned eighteen. Dan had kept an eye on her ever since.

"Working a case." He opened his phone, pulled up a photo of Phil and handed it over. "Ever see this guy?"

"Is that that chef that was murdered?"

"Yep. He ever come in here?"

"Not here, but I've seen him around."

"Where?"

"Saw him at a little dive in Placerville. Hangman's Tavern. He was playing kissy-face with an older woman. Very attractive in a cheap way—I should talk," she said, hiking up her neckline and shaking her blond mane. She placed a tall one in front of Dan and scurried to the other end of the bar to take an order. When she returned, she placed a bowl of club mix next to Dan's beer.

"Are you sure it was him?"

"Positive. It's a small town. Who hasn't been to Ésquisito? Plus, I had seen him working out at the gym down the street. It's a block from my apartment. Everyone knew who he was. He was like a big deal around here."

"Did you happen to get a good look at the woman he was with?"

"Pretty sure. You got photos? I can take a look."

Dan scrolled through his phone, searching for women who appeared older. "What about this one?"

"Hell no. She used to anchor for one of those offbeat news programs. She's dating a friend of mine, a female friend."

The detective produced another. "What about her?"

"No. This woman had dark hair. Could've been a wig, but I doubt it. The woman was well put together."

The only shots Dan had left were of couples posing with Phil. "Anyone here?"

Trina grabbed the phone. "Let me see," she said, expanding the size of the picture with two fingers. "Not this one." She swiped to the next. "Nope." She glanced down to the end of the bar. "Be right with you," she called to a newcomer. She scrolled through several more images until she said, "This one. Her hair was longer, but it's her."

Dan tucked his phone back into his pocket, tossed a twenty on the bar, and blew Trina a kiss. "See ya 'round, beautiful."

"Always a pleasure, Detective."

***

Traffic around town would be hellacious for the next hour. Dan headed home to have a little dinner and do some research. When he opened his email, he saw a note from Ben:

> Dan,
>
> I sent the department an update on Phillip Maltese's autopsy. I wanted to share a few of my notes with you personally. Keep in mind that this is partially supposition and not yet proven.
>
> The fatal wounds were made by a 9 ½-inch slicing knife. The victim was stabbed numerous times in the abdomen, piercing retroperitoneal organs at different angles: left kidney, duodenum, small bowel and intestines. The assumed murder weapon found at the scene matches the wounds. However, the prints on the handle belonged to the victim. (It's not likely he stabbed himself multiple times in the back.) As I mentioned, my granddaughter graduated from culinary school. Most professional chefs own a set of knives with micro-carbide steel blades that have a katana edge for scalpel-like sharpness. The blades are hand-honed using the Honbazuke method to get an exceptionally sharp 9.5 to 12-degree angle.
>
> I established his time of death on Wednesday, April 17, approximately 2 A.M.
>
> We also found cat hair on his clothing and narrow abrasions on his left cheek that appear to have come

from pointed objects an inch apart and unevenly spaced. One of the lines was incomplete. My first impression? Someone broke a nail. Don't hold me to that one!

Hope this gives you something to go on. Good luck finding your killer(s). —Ben

Dan placed his dinner back into the fridge and dashed to his car. Ben's email whirled in his brain. The evidence suggested he was on the right track.

***

He circled twice to find a place to park. Ésquisito was packed. Dan remembered Giovanni saying he had a big party booked for the evening, but this couldn't wait. The back door was ajar. He slipped inside.

"I can't talk to you right now, Detective."

"I only need a minute."

Giovanni wiped his hands on his apron. "You have thirty seconds."

Dan produced a photo of Giovanni posing with Phil and a couple in the foyer of the restaurant several years before the Covid closure.

Giovanni's eyes grew large. "What is this?"

"Who are they?"

"That's my realtor, John Fredericks, and his wife Ruby. They're good people—not killers!" He paused to rein in his temper. "Your thirty seconds are up." He showed Dan his back instead of the door.

Dan dropped his phone into his pocket and left the same way he came in, nearly tripping on a black-and-white cat sprawled across the concrete step.

He slipped behind the steering wheel and called the station. "I need an address for a John Fredericks, he's a realtor."

Twenty minutes later, Dan pulled up to a home in the Fab 40s. He admired the manicured lawn, the perfectly pruned mulberry trees, hedges, and pristine flower gardens. He had forgotten how the other half lived and immediately remembered why he wasn't among them. He rang the bell and waited, noticing a white cat chasing a lizard across the retaining wall to his left.

A beautiful brunette dressed in a casual halter dress answered the door. Her tan skin glistened in the backlight coming from the French doors behind her. Dan could see a pool from where he stood. He smelled barbeque and saw wafts of smoke coming from the same direction. The woman had a drink in her hand. He guessed it was a margarita by the shape of the glass.

"Can I help you?" she asked.

The detective produced his badge. "Detective Dan Calian, Sacramento Sheriff's Department. May I come in?" He watched her pale as she unlatched the lock on the storm door.

"My husband is in the backyard, let me —"

"Before you get your husband, I'd like to ask you a few questions. I am investigating the death of Phillip Maltese. How well did you know him?" He found it interesting that Ruby's reaction mimicked Stephanie's. Her fingers danced across her clavicle, suggesting intimacy. Her reply reminded him of his first car. It sputtered until he gave it a little gas, then purred.

"I-I didn't know him well at all. I mean, I knew who he was and had a couple of photos taken with him and the owner, Giovanni. But I wouldn't say we were friends."

Just then, John entered the room carrying a platter full of barbequed chicken. The aroma made Dan's stomach go nuts. He flashed on the frozen dinner he had deposited back in the freezer before he left.

John's face registered his surprise. "What's going on?"

Dan introduced himself, showed his badge, and continued with his questioning. "I was just asking your wife how well she knew Phillip Maltese." Dan noticed John wince before he replied.

"We met Phil when we met Giovanni through a real estate deal. I sold Giovanni the property for Ésquisito's. We've been dining there for about eight years." John set the platter down on the dining room table "How exactly did he die?"

Dan caught a glimpse of the wife wringing her hands. He looked right at her when he said, "He was stabbed—numerous times." He watched her eyes widen, her nostrils flare. He imagined her ears were ringing from the adrenaline rush of hearing those words.

"Are you okay, Mrs. Fredericks?"

She pulled out a dining room chair and sat down. John rushed to her side, bent down on one knee and searched her eyes. "Baby?"

She composed herself and rose. "Bad news on an empty stomach—that's all." She walked to the front door and opened it. "If you have no further questions, Detective Calian, our dinner is getting cold."

John escorted Dan to his car. "This may be nothing, but when we went to dinner at Ésquisito the night Giovanni reopened, I opened my menu and saw a red splat under the Fork and Knife section. I thought it was odd that the staff hadn't wiped it off. It didn't look like ketchup…"

"What do you think it was?"

"Maybe blood? I set it aside and ordered off my wife's menu."

"Interesting. I'll check into it." Dan tapped his temple. "I almost forgot to ask—do you have any pets?"

John shook his head. "My wife is attracted to snakes. I like cats. Not a compatible combination."

Dan pulled away from the house with mixed feelings. His gut told him the wife was hiding something, and perhaps the husband, too. Was the menu thing a bone to throw him off course?

***

Dan tried a different approach this time at Ésquisito. He walked in the front door and spoke with the hostess, Mandy.

"I know this is an odd request, but can I see your menus?"

"What for?"

"When I was here opening night, I placed a very important business card inside my menu and forgot to take it out. I'm really hoping it's still in there."

"You may be in luck," she said. "We wipe our menus down on Wednesdays before we open."

"Do you use the same menus every night?"

"No, we rotate them." She held up one finger and disappeared into a small room next to the coat check area. She returned with a stack of menus. "Let's look through these. I believe they're from last Friday."

Dan opened each menu, hoping to get lucky. He kept an eye on the hostess, waiting for a reaction should she find the red splotch before he did—that's if it really existed, which it did.

"Ew," she said. "Glad the boss didn't see this."

"May I?" Dan took the offensive item from her hand. When he was sure he had what he was looking for, he reached in his pocket for his badge.

***

Dan sent the menu to the lab. The results were conclusive. Along with the tip he had received from Ben, he had his answer.

***

Giovanni perched on a metal chair across from the detective and a deputy. Dan held up a knife sealed in a plastic bag. "Recognize this?"

Giovanni's gaze dropped to the floor.

Dan placed the bag on the table. "You want to tell me what happened?"

"You think I stabbed him?"

"The knife we found at Phil's matches his wounds. Nine-and-a-half-inch blade, SG2 micro-carbide steel, katana edge, hand-honed to a razor sharp twelve-degree angle..." Dan took notice of the perspiration beading on Giovanni's brow. "I'll ask again. What happened?"

Giovanni's lips tightened. He didn't budge. Dan sat on the edge of the table, leaned in, and dropped his tone. "We have the building's security footage. I think you went over to Phil's to show him the new menu. When you got there, you heard Stephanie inside his apartment. Maybe you pressed your ear to the door. Maybe they were having a lover's quarrel..."

Giovanni clenched his teeth.

"Maybe Phil was saying awful, cruel things." When Dan was sure he had struck a nerve, he picked up the evidence bag.

Giovanni turned away.

"When my men collected the murder weapon, they didn't just collect the nine-and-a-half inch slicing knife, they collected the whole set. We also collected an identical set of knives from Ésquisito. Do you want to know what we found?"

Giovanni buried his head in his hands.

"You switched knives, Mr. Gaballo. We can prove it. What I want to know is why? Why did you kill him? Why didn't you just fire him?" Giovanni looked up, his expression weary, his woeful voice laced with rage.

"He was always bragging about his conquests, including my realtor's wife," he snarled. "I couldn't—"

"He knew you were in love with Stephanie, didn't he?"

Giovanni's shoulders slumped forward. Dan continued.

"I'll bet that made you very angry."

"He promised he would stay away from her."

"What I want to know is, who stabbed him first?"

Giovanni straightened his posture and glared at the detective, his eyes hard, cold, deadly. "I did."

***

Dan re-entered the interrogation room down the hall from where he had questioned Giovanni. He dropped the evidence bag holding the knife on the table.

"You weren't expecting Giovanni to show up, were you?"

Stephanie shook her head.

"Did he know about you and Phil?"

"No."

"Is that what set him off? Seeing you two together?"

"No." She dropped her gaze. "Giovanni asked him what was going on? Phil said, 'Nothing important.' He said I was just another piece of meat to him."

"What I want to know is who stabbed Phil first?"

Stephanie's red, swollen eyes lifted to meet his. "I did." Fresh tears streamed down her cheeks. Her shoulders shook. Her lower lip trembled. She bowed her head, her voice barely a whisper, "I thought he loved me."

***

Dan wrapped up the case before midnight. He marveled at how easy it was to go astray when it came to love. He knew first-hand what it was like to feel deeply for someone, what it was like to be betrayed. Maybe if he had had one of those fancy knives ... Nah. Wasn't in his nature.

The Tank House BBQ & Bar was on his way home. They were open until two A.M. If he was lucky, Trina would be there. He felt like celebrating.

THE COMPETITION

Susan Egan

"He's supposed to love me," Remy said. "Me!" This time, she pounded her chest with her fist.

"I'm so sorry," I said, shrugging my shoulders. I had also witnessed Lucas's duplicity and had no ready answer. I could only comfort her.

"Who was that thing he was with anyway? Have you ever seen lipstick that red?" Remy said. She stared at the third finger of her left hand, where she once wore a diamond, surrounded by sapphires. Not now. Not after what she had witnessed an hour ago. He had broken a date with her, saying he was in the midst of perfecting his latest recipe when all along he was busy two-timing her.

"I have no idea," I said, averting my eyes from her beet-red face. "Maybe she's also a contestant. It seems the whole world was invited to participate."

Every year the organizers of the Farm to Fork Festival held a contest, looking for the next culinary sensation. It wasn't confined to only California residents which explained why Remy and Lucas had flown across the United States to Sacramento. Lucas—according to Remy—had called it their pre-honeymoon, but I wondered if it was an excuse.

"You can't lose your focus now," I said. "You've got too much at stake. You can deal with Lucas later. Forget him." Sage advice, but I hadn't seen my future vanish before my eyes.

"I've just spent the last five years of my life with him." Remy was too angry to cry. Maybe later when she was alone, she would surrender to her emotions. "How can I go on?"

"You flew from New York for this. Are you going to throw your ambitions away because of one man's roving eye?"

It was worse than that. She had caught Lucas in a rather compromising position with The Thing. He had tried to explain, but Remy had stormed out of the bar.

"I'm returning to New York. Tonight," Remy, patting the perspiration from her forehead with an already saturated tissue, said. "I have my ticket. All I've got to do is get to the airport, rebook, and fly home." True, she could arrive in New York in time for breakfast.

"But you came here to compete and to win. You've auditioned for this contest for too many years to just give up and run away because your fiancée cannot keep his jeans zippered…"

"Former fiancée."

"Whatever." My lips were a straight line. "Your choice, but I would reconsider if I were you."

"But, Celia, you're not me. You weren't the one hurt," she said. "Please give me a ride to the airport. I can't bear to call an Uber. Not when I need the support of a friend."

My car was parked outside the café where we had fled after the incident. All I had to do was agree, but I knew where this was headed. Remy would forever regret this decision if she didn't compete, a dream of hers since our college days. The prestige of winning was just too seductive.

"I can't. I told Declan I would be home to tuck the kids into bed. I've already stayed out later than I expected." I glanced at my watch.

"Please. I can't face the ride to the airport alone. I'm so upset, I'm so mixed up…"

I hated when she played on my sympathies. As I was about to surrender, Declan texted me. "I have to go. Seriously. The kids are waiting…"

Remy pouted, but I didn't intend to give in to her request.

"See you tomorrow," I said instead and squeezed her hand.

***

"I'm glad you reconsidered," I said, hugging Remy. "You look refreshed." She seemed calmer as she settled into my car.

"Melatonin. Works every time," she said. "I decided you were right. I've wanted to compete in this contest since senior year. I can't let a mere bump in the road destroy my dream of winning."

An unfaithful fiancée was a bump? Her cavalier attitude towards Lucas surprised me. No one recovered from a broken engagement overnight, especially after a long-term relationship.

"I went back to the hotel and tweaked my recipe. Or should I say refined? Anyway, they say creativity springs from the depths of despair, right?"

"I suppose." I had never heard such nonsense, but I wasn't about to argue the point.

"The Thing can have him. Something must have been obviously missing in our relationship, and whatever it was, The Thing provides it. I can't compete. Good luck to her is all I've got to say."

Bravado? Comforting herself? I wanted to believe Remy, but somehow it sounded hollow, like she was trying to convince herself. Yet, I was in favor of whatever would get her through the competition.

"Do you need a taster? I promise to tell you the truth," I said as I maneuvered through the streets of Sacramento. Remy had rented a kitchen where she could perfect her recipe.

"Sure, why not? "

After circling the block for what seemed like the hundredth time, I found a spot.

"Why don't you come back in a couple of hours? That should give me enough time to cook." She smiled a little too broadly for someone who had probably spent hours crying last night.

"Sure, I have to teach my classes, then run a few errands. I told the kids I would bring home cupcakes for dessert tonight."

***

I had exchanged my apron long ago for a job as a college professor. I had planned to visit Vienna after college graduation and learn the art of pastry making, but before I could board a flight, I was offered a fellowship in classical languages. I regarded cooking as fun, but I never saw it as a viable career choice. When it came to the art of cooking, Remy was always better and more ambitious than I. After college, she attended a culinary school in New York and then jetted off to Europe to study at whatever school offered her a scholarship. We had kept in touch, but I hadn't seen her since my wedding ten years ago and was elated when she texted that she was coming to California to compete in the Farm to Fork contest.

"Smells heavenly," I said, as I walked into her kitchen.

"I'm not sure that's a compliment. We don't know what heaven smells like," she said, as she stirred a pot of sauce. "Here, taste this." She offered me a spoonful.

"I've never tasted such a sauce," I said. I could distinguish the mushrooms, tomatoes, and olives, but she had added something that had my taste buds soaring skyward. "A secret ingredient?"

"The herbs?" she said. "It's the usual. Basil, garlic, oregano, rosemary, thyme … I bought them in Italy during the summer."

"No, it's something else." I grabbed a second spoon and dipped into the sauce again. "So creamy, but it's not heavy cream. It's something else."

"Good. My idea is working. You really don't detect what it is?" I shook my head.

"I've used cream in the past, but I read somewhere that I should use a dab of cream cheese instead. It's different. Always good to give the judges something to think about. Don't you agree, Celia? You were always my best critic…"

"Certainly," I said, suddenly nostalgic for our college years and when we spent our weekends experimenting with recipes and debated which way our career paths would veer.

"I don't know why you pursued dead languages over culinary school. You would've been happier creating recipes rather than grading papers."

"Perhaps, but need I remind you that we met in an ancient history class? And that we both bonded over *I, Claudius*?" I said. We had found the DVDs in the library and had watched them until we could recite the dialogue from memory.

"How can I forget the villainesses Livia, Messalina, and Agrippina? Such treachery, such debauchery," she said, stirring her sauce. "Still, I'd rather cook than translate. Doesn't Caesar, Tacitus, and Suetonius get boring after a while? How many times can you teach them?"

"It's a living, and I'm home when I need to be for the kids. That's something." Remy's focus had returned. Soon, she would relegate Lucas to the dustbin of former lovers. I was relieved at her turnaround.

"If teaching makes you happy…" she said, a wistful expression crossing her face. "Still, cooking is much more creative."

"What time do you have to be at the venue tomorrow? Do you need a ride?" I said. I hadn't told Remy, but I had cleared most of my schedule for her. Prescient of me as she needed my support now more than ever.

"Around eight. Does that work for you?"

"Of course, and if it doesn't, I'll make it."

***

The Farm to Fork organizers had rented a tent to accommodate the participants for their annual contest. This year, as our local newspaper had reported, had seen a record number of applicants. In the interest of fairness, Gabrielle Fontaine, the chief judge, had accepted more than usual to compete. Although the contest awarded three prizes, only one would garner a spread in the esteemed magazine *La Bonne Cuisine* and a feature on its Food Network show, a dream for budding chefs.

I pulled into one of the last spaces in the parking lot and helped Remy haul her supplies into the tent.

"We have preassigned spots. I hope my kitchen isn't near Lucas. Talk about uncomfortable," she said, steering her cart through the lot. "We requested neighboring stoves, and they said they would accommodate us. But that was before the incident."

"It'll be okay," I said, but I gulped. Remy felt enough pressure to succeed. She didn't need his presence to further unnerve her.

"You always put a positive spin on everything, Celia, even when there isn't one," Remy said, her lips pursed. "I promise I'll be fine. I won't let Lucas derail me."

I side-eyed Remy. I wasn't sure I believed her. I never remembered her getting over a break-up overnight when we were in college, but perhaps the intervening years had changed her. We become wiser with age…

"Can you pick me up at seven tonight? The actual competition is tomorrow, and then the gala is the next night. I want you to come as my guest. There's going to be a tasting."

"Sure." I rued the day I had agreed to act as her taxi service for the duration of the festival, but I reminded myself it was temporary. And she needed me. "Are you sure that you don't want me to help you set up?"

She paused to consider my offer. "I don't want to impose, but if you can spare forty-five minutes, I would appreciate it."

I didn't have the time—three kids and teaching full-time present daily challenges—but I wanted to reassure myself that she could prepare for the competition in peace.

"This way," she said, flailing in the direction of the tent.

As we entered, we were given a map, detailing where each chef's kitchen was located. Remy's was in the center, a prime location, and we wended our way through the aisles in search of it. I didn't bother to look for Lucas and his kitchen.

"Safe so far," she whispered as she did a three-sixty. "Hopefully, he's in Oregon by now."

Wishful thinking. No one would give up their place in a prestigious contest. But safe is a relative term. Let Remy believe that fantasy.

"Oh, there he is. He's an aisle over, and he's with that ... thing," she said, recoiling.

"Forget him. Remember why you came to Sacramento," I said through teeth gritted so hard they hurt. "Are you going to let him ruin your chances at a spread in that magazine? Or a segment on the Food Network?"

"No, and to prove it, I'll go and say hello to him. Tell him that there are no hard feelings. He wants to win as much as I do. His signature dish is some duck thing we had when we visited Ireland last year. He fell in love with it and asked the chef for the recipe. Lucas pled with him, but he politely refused. Somehow, he replicated it and did a near-perfect job. Sadly, for me. He's probably my strongest competition."

Judging from the number of contestants, I deemed that unlikely.

"Please don't start with a defeatist attitude. That isn't you."

"No, I won't. Still, the contest won't be a cakewalk, no pun intended," she said, surveying her surroundings. "As good as my recipe is, there's always someone with a better one."

I nodded. "Perhaps. Are you okay with me leaving? I've got to get back to the kids before they destroy the house." I exaggerated, but I couldn't stay and feared more drama. I knew well how Remy operated.

"Sure, Celia." She air-kissed me. "I've got to be an adult about this. Lucas may have destroyed one dream., but I'm not letting him destroy the other." She opened a crate and began removing her cookware. "See you later? Is eight convenient?"

"Of course," I said, lying. It was the kids' bedtime, but Declan could handle them. "Break a leg."

***

"How did it go?" The aroma in the tent was intoxicating. I could smell tomatoes, garlic, onions, beef, chicken, and a whole array of spices. I had given up experimenting with recipes when I became a professor and then started a family. I counted myself lucky if I could manage a new pasta dish once a month.

"Swimmingly. Gabrielle Fontaine and her entourage visited each chef and sampled our recipes. I could tell that Gabrielle was impressed with my dish even though she didn't say much. I could just tell she liked it." She paused for dramatic effect. "I glanced over when she stopped by to speak with Lucas. She didn't have the same reaction as she did with me. I'm taking that as a good omen," she said, unable to suppress the snark. Whatever. I wasn't weighing in on Remy's assessment.

"Same time tomorrow?" I said, trying to hustle her out of the tent. I knew how these affairs went. Everyone wanted to share their experiences, hoping this would give them an edge.

"Earlier than today. Around seven thirty?"

I grimaced, but I would make it work. The festival's end was approaching.

***

"I went to the market last night after you dropped me off," Remy said, settling into the passenger's seat. "I bought…" And she detailed the number of items she had purchased: cooking accessories, spices, and even a chef's hat. "My credit card isn't happy."

But I was. Seeing her relaxed reassured me. Only three nights ago, I had seen her in the depths of despair.

"I forgot to ask you. Did you speak to…"

"Yes. I said I would. You would've been proud of me. I told Lucas that I was over him, and I would return the ring after the contest if he wanted it back."

Lucas had given her a one carat ring. It dwarfed mine, but then Declan was poor when we became engaged.

The tent bustled as we entered. I remembered those days. Some chefs practically lived by their stove when in the midst of a competition. So much riding on one recipe...

"Hi." Lucas had crept up on us. I hadn't realized he was there until I heard him greet us.

"Oh, hi," Remy said. I saw both sadness and anger cross her face. Lucas's timing was off. I wondered why he couldn't have waited until after the contest was over to cheat on Remy. I still worried she would decompress and her creativity in the kitchen would fail her.

"I want to wish you luck. I know how long you've waited to compete. May the best chef win…"

What? Did I detect a note of insincerity? I didn't know Lucas, but I could judge a person's character. I had witnessed that scene, but because I didn't know the history of their relationship, I couldn't assign blame.

"You as well." She returned to organizing her kitchen utensils and ingredients.

"Will you be at the tasting and gala tomorrow night?" Lucas asked.

"Yes. I'm looking forward to tasting everyone's recipes. Aren't you?" she said, tying a much-loved apron around her waist. It was worn, and I hoped the judges wouldn't penalize her for her attire.

"I wouldn't miss it. It's part of the fun in competing." He winked at her. She pretended not to notice, but I was sure his action stung.

"Looks like we're starting," he said, grabbing and then squeezing her hand.

"Yes," she said, shooing him away. "Time to get serious. Homemade pasta doesn't make itself."

***

"I wasn't expecting you back so soon. Weren't you helping Remy set up?" Declan said as he brushed a kiss across my lips. "I told the kids we're having pizza for dinner because you're too busy with the festival."

"Sorry. I should've told you." I said, yawning. "The contest organizers don't want any spectators hanging around. They must think we'll give them an unfair advantage."

"If they only knew how you cook…" Declan laughed, but it wasn't malicious.

"I was good once," I said. I had never regretted the day I had given up my former life for marriage and academia. "When I pick Remy up later, I'm sure I'll get a detailed account of her day."

"Then she's okay after the breakup? Wow, the quickest recovery I've ever seen. I didn't know women rebounded so well. If that had happened to me, I'd be licking my wounds for months, if not years."

"I told her to remain focused, and she has heeded my advice so far. I keep thinking that it's all a facade. That I'm not seeing something…" I had dismissed such thoughts. If Remy was acting for my benefit, as well as the judges, so be it.

"She's a big girl. It's not your problem."

Still, I couldn't help wondering.

***

"It's almost midnight. Are you pulling an all-nighter?" Declan said. He put aside the thriller he was reading and patted the other side of the bed, inviting me in. "Can't you do that in the morning?"

"I could but…" I sifted again through the papers and books on my desk. I had assigned several passages from Suetonius to my students and wanted to review the text, but I couldn't find my translation anywhere. "Did you see my copy of *The Twelve Caesars*?"

"I saw it in the car this morning. Did you look downstairs? Or maybe you left it at school?"

"I guess." I was meticulous when it came to keeping track of my textbooks. I always made sure when I taught a particular course that I carried the book to and from school every day. I often referred to it when I prepared my lectures. "I'll ask Remy in the morning if she saw it. Strange, though."

"You're tired. Come to bed. You can always ad-lib your way through your lecture. Your students won't even notice."

"Maybe." Yet, I had never fooled them before.

***

"Sorry, I picked this up by accident yesterday." Remy snapped her seat belt on and then handed me my book. "I hope it didn't cause you any angst last night. I probably should have called to let you know."

"Thanks. At least it's safe and sound." I turned around and shoved my copy of *The Twelve Caesars* into my knapsack. "It forced me to change part of this morning's lecture. I had planned to start on Claudius, but I'll just continue on with Caligula. No shortage of things to say about him," I said, pulling away from the curb. "Are you ready for today?"

"Claudius met a terrible end if I remember correctly, didn't he?" she said, ignoring my question. "Something about mushrooms?"

"Yes, his wife, Agrippina, supposedly fed him poisoned mushrooms from her own plate because she wanted her son, Nero, to succeed him as emperor, but who knows if it's true? Suetonius was a gossip."

"Oh," she said. "Didn't all the Caesars kill off their rivals? But in answer to your question, yes. An all-day affair: announcement of the winners, the tastings, and finally, the gala. If the aromas are anything to go by, I should gain five pounds by the end of the evening. You're coming, right? I reserved a ticket for Declan, too."

"I'm not sure about Declan. He's too wrapped up in baseball and supervising the kids' homework, but I plan on coming," I said, pulling into the lot.

"Around six," she said, getting out of the car.

"Sure," I said.

***

I entered the tent, hoping to catch Remy before the evening festivities began, but I didn't see her anywhere. The tent was mobbed, as this was the festival's premiere event.

"Here you are. I was afraid you wouldn't show up," Remy said, smiling and then hugging me. In this crowd, I was surprised she had found me.

"I wouldn't miss this," I said. Something didn't seem right about Remy—her fake gaiety. No one was this happy, especially after a broken engagement. I agreed with Declan: no one recovered virtually overnight.

"The tastings are first, and then the winners are announced. Please make sure you sample my dish," she said. "I've got to go." And she rushed off.

I wandered through the aisles tasting some dishes. As a vegetarian, I declined all the meat dishes, but there was still plenty to choose from. I steered clear of the desserts even though they looked delectable. On a whim, I gravitated towards Lucas's table. He had a crowd gathered around him, all oohing and aahing over his duck.

"Would you like a sample?" he said.

"Only if you have something vegetarian. Sorry." The aroma emanating from the table made me heady.

"I made a vegetable accompaniment. You can taste that," Lucas said, handing me a small plate.

"Sure," I said, feeling disloyal to Remy.

"Oh, here you are." Remy had seemed to appear out of the ozone. She held in her hands two petite plates of her current signature dish, homemade whole wheat pasta made with mushrooms, tomatoes, and olives. She claimed its secret ingredient, which she would only divulge to me, accounted for its distinct taste. "I wanted you to sample it before it was gone."

I turned and took a plate from her.

"And this is for you, Lucas. May the best chef win."

"I absolutely can't wait to try your dish." Lucas reached for the plate, but Remy waved his hands away.

"Here," she said, scooping up a generous forkful of her pasta and vegetables. "It's to die for."

I had turned away for a moment. I was distracted by a group of teenagers cackling over a tableful of different flavors of cannolis. Despite my vow not to touch any desserts, I was tempted to try either the hazelnut or raspberry varieties. I was about to reach for one when I saw Remy place her pasta inside Lucas's mouth.

Die for?

Some people claim that one sees their whole life flash before their eyes when facing death. I wasn't the one about to die, but I did see the past five days unfold before my eyes: Lucas two-timing Remy, her protestations that she was over Lucas, the conversation about how the emperor Claudius had died, allegedly by his wife feeding him poison mushrooms, and then the missing volume of Suetonius.

I dropped my cannoli onto the floor as I lunged for Lucas.

"Nooooooo," I screamed. "It's poi…"

Yet, I knew I was too late. I stared in horror as a writhing Lucas crumpled to the ground.

MIDTOWN MARKET GIRL

Karen Harrington

We sat in a tight wreath around Marge. This was the way of the Oakdale wives. Marge wasn't going to escape until she was done. Each of us averted the other's eyes. Marge moaned, sobbed, and begged. But we held fast to the circle. Though our intentions were good, I wondered if Marge felt like a caged animal. She didn't look comfortable.

"I can't breathe," she sobbed. "Why?"

Her pain was so raw and sharp that it couldn't help but nick those around her. I felt the tiny cuts of loss dig into my own skin. How could I escape? I glanced backward at the table to see if anyone new had entered—someone who might come and take my place in the human fence. There wasn't. Marge wiped at her eyes with a soggy tissue. Could I get up and replace it? Would that be acceptable? I couldn't be sure. Since we'd moved to Oakdale, I'd seen how small and tight the community was. They had their own ways. After two years, I still felt like an outsider.

My phone buzzed—a text from my husband, Stan.

Come help with the coffee.

Sweet relief, I was liberated. "Stan needs me," I said, excusing myself.

Marge's kitchen was large and merry. She had one of those fancy coffee makers that grinds and brews—an all-in-one.

Stan was having trouble getting it to work, or so he said. I think he knew the living room ritual had gotten to me.

"S'pose someone will need to deal with Marge and Jim's peaches," he said.

"She can miss this once," I said.

"Already missed last Saturday when Jim was at the hospital," Stan said. "She's got to keep her spot or she'll lose it. They worked so hard to get into Midtown."

"You're probably right." The Midtown Farmers Market in Sacramento was competitive. They'd been on the waitlist for more than a year.

"I was thinking we could volunteer," he said. "We haven't been to the city in a while."

He winked at me. I loved my husband. He knew I wasn't built for sitting and grieving. I had to stay in motion to outrun my thoughts, which trended toward the dark side. Thoughts of our daughter always pressed in. She was once a young rebel who managed to pry open her enclosure with the help of an unpleasant boy. One night, the unpleasant boy had driven drunk with her. He lived, she didn't. The ache and the injustice stalked me daily.

The coffee began percolating from Marge's machine, and the scent reminded me of my lost girl. I pictured her in her ponytail behind the barista counter—a bittersweet memory.

After we lost her, Stan stopped teaching at UC Davis, got a job at Modesto Junior College, and moved us to the Central Valley to a small pecan orchard. Down the road, there was a man who bred sheep. Further on, Marge and Jim's fruit orchard. Out here there was always something that needed pulling, planting, paint, or water. What we didn't know about farming, we learned fast. We called it the temporary farm cure for despair.

Stan conveyed our plan to Marge, and the next morning at six a.m., we loaded our truck with Marge's market table, tablecloths, signage, two hand trucks, dozens of crates of sweet peaches, and boxes of green baskets that bore the label Mim's Peaches, Mim being the combination of their names. We aimed the truck along Highway 99 toward Sacramento. The Midtown Farmers Market opened at eight and we had to be there at least thirty minutes before opening.

We arrived amid the bustle and jostle of dozens of vendors along 20th Street. The sky was a washed-out blue and the air was mild. Stan found our stall assignment and we unloaded. The tent went up quickly. I spread the royal blue checkered tablecloth, arranged the crates of peaches, and hung Mim's signage. Then, bundled peaches into green baskets, three dollars per.

The table next to us had scores of bell peppers, cucumbers, and broccoli. Another table teemed with strawberries. I'd forgotten how much color and scent filled the market.

This volunteering business had been a good idea.

"I'm going to run back for the chairs," Stan said. "You'll be here when I get back, won't you?"

"Very funny," I said, smiling.

The place filled with families and dogs. No sooner had I sold eight baskets of peaches when a man leaned across the table and got uncomfortably close to my face.

"I'm going to leave her here for a minute."

I backed away. The man was narrow as a ribbon. His bony hand rested on the head of a green-eyed girl with a worrying scratch on her cheek.

"What? No, you can't do that," I said.

The Ribbon Man disappeared into the crowd.

Wait!" I called.

The girl had a blank expression, no fear or anxiety. I guessed her to be around eight or nine.

"He'll be back eventually," she said. "He does this every Saturday."

"What? He leaves you? Alone?"

"He finds decent people at the market."

"Where's your mother?"

The girl answered with a shrug. And then, "Last week, I was at a food truck, and it wasn't nice."

I had to tend to a customer. The girl moved behind the table and stood next to me like she belonged there. A trail of her body odor climbed through the air.

"Who's this?" Stan said when he got back.

"A man just left the child and ran off," I told him. "Should we call the police? She says he does this every Saturday."

Stan brought his hand to his chin and went into his solution-mode, one he'd honed as a teacher.

"The thing to do is wait this out for a bit before we get any authorities involved. Like as not, he'll be back."

"He will," said the girl, looking up at Stan. "The only time he missed, he said he was sorry and wouldn't do it again."

This was all too concerning. "Where do you live?"

The girl shrugged again. "Between places, but mostly outside near the corral. Can I have a peach?"

Stan took out his knife and sliced a peach in quarters. At the point of exchange between his hand and hers, Stan asked her name.

"June," she said. She devoured the peach slice and then another one.

"Why don't you sit back here, June," I said, pointing to one of the chairs. We sold a dozen baskets in a rush. I asked June if she could help me assemble more peaches into the Mim's baskets. She seemed to delight in this, counting from one to five as she went.

I plucked a battered peach from one of her baskets and replaced it with a good one. "If you find ones like this, set them aside."

"For the dumpster?" she asked.

"Well," I said, stopping short of agreeing or disagreeing.

Stan gave me a look that signaled he'd heard what she said. I wiped dripping juice from June's chin. She couldn't stop nibbling on the samples.

"What happened to your face?" I asked.

"I don't want to tell you," June said.

"Okay."

"You'll be grossed out."

"Think so?"

She whispered to me. "It was a rat."

My eyes shot up. I didn't know what to say to this cruel fact. And I didn't want to make her feel bad. "I hope you punched him back."

June laughed.

"You'd be a good mama," she said.

Stan swept in before I could catch my breath. "That's right, June. She's a good mama."

I swallowed hard.

A rush of sales carried us for another hour. I kept scanning the street for June's father. She seemed nonplussed and only slipped away from me for a moment to grab a cherry sample from the nearby vendor. I kept my eye trained on her as she wove through the crowd. That's when I saw him. The unpleasant boyfriend. His hair cropped short now. My stomach dropped.

"Stan," I said, nodding across the lane.

"The boy," Stan said sharply.

The boy had a new girl with him, and they looked irritatingly happy. It was hard to take my gaze from his face. Nothing about him showed his mistake, and I guessed I wanted some hideous scar or deformity to remind him daily. To make people ask him: *What happened there?*

The boyfriend had never talked to us after. Never.

"Why are you all crinkly?" June was at my side again.

"I saw something sour," I said. "Someone sour."

"I could go throw a peach at them for you," June beamed. "One of the dumpster ones."

The unpleasant boy vanished in the crowd—a near miss.

"That would've been funny," I told her.

The park thinned, and a couple of vendors who'd sold out began dismantling—still no sign of the neglectful Ribbon Man. My mind raced. It was nearing time to get the police involved, though part of me felt sad about where the girl might end up for the night.

But then here came her father, shuffling and stumbling and calling her name. By the time he reached us, he had to steady himself against June's back. He was drunk. So this was his Saturday routine? Getting smashed during the market hours?

"Come on, Junie."

"I helped sell peaches today."

"So what," he said. "Come on now."

"But wait, are you all right?" I asked. "Do you need to sit down?" I wanted to accuse him, but I stopped short. People turned violent for nothing these days. You had to be careful.

"Do I need to sit down?" he asked sharply. "Hell no. Now let's go, June!"

June slammed into me with a hug that only weighed a feather and then let go just as quick. She took her father's shaking hand and looked back at us.

"Bye, Mim's peach people."

"But…" I tried to force words out. What were we doing?

Stan put a comforting hand to my shoulder. "He'll probably go sleep it off somewhere. You heard her. They're between places. Homeless."

"That's still no good."

Then I grabbed two peach baskets, filled them, and raced toward June. My soul had to do something.

"June," I called. She stopped and turned as I caught up with them, nearly breathless.

"Here, you earned these," I said. I put a basket against the man's chest and offered the other to her.

Her face glowed with happiness.

"These are the best, Daddy," she said, smiling. "Leave me at the fruit places from now on."

He looked back to me, guilty. "I only left you this once, June. This once."

June knew better than to reply.

They walked away, and I stood there until I couldn't see them anymore as they wove behind the food trucks.

Stan and I quickly loaded up and prepared for the drive back to Oakdale. He handed me the keys with a nod. He sensed I needed to drive so my mind wouldn't linger on anything but the road. Even for a short time.

The traffic was thick as we rounded Stockton Boulevard toward Highway 99. I turned up the radio and hummed along to a country tune.

"Let's get a coffee on the way," I said.

"Careful now. Do you see that?" Stan said.

"I see him," I said. "Oh, God."

A car ahead of us was speeding and weaving heavily, unable to stay in its lane. It clipped another car, jerked hard right and then smashed head-on into a concrete light pole. It all happened so fast that I'd barely had time to think, only to react as I swerved to a sudden stop on the grassy shoulder area, narrowly missing a man walking by the road. The car that had been behind me smashed into the one in front. We'd slipped the trap.

"You okay," Stan asked.

I wasn't sure. I rolled down my window for air. Then there was the screeching of countless tires and people running toward the disaster from the homeless camp, and Stan was calling 911. I could hear his voice through the slow-motion fog. I got out of the truck and advanced toward the injured vehicle that was already hemorrhaging fluids and steam. An empty green basket lay on the road. I told myself, *That could be anyone's. It didn't have to be Mim's.* But near it, there was her small form splayed awkwardly. Around her head, a halo of peaches and broken glass. A thin man with a bloodied face pulled himself through the window and slumped to the pavement like a wet sack.

My dark thoughts pressed down heavily as I processed what I couldn't bear to look at. The Ribbon Man was alive. June was still and lifeless. The terror turned to rage in an instant. I looked around and saw, just beyond the road, a Golden Corral restaurant. So they lived here. Suddenly, I was both clear and insane at once because I knew I was going to kill the man. There was time to do it before the authorities arrived. The man could just be another casualty in the pile-up.

Stan was in my periphery, talking to someone on the phone. Another witness was on the road, also talking to someone. I moved back to our truck and started the engine. If no one walked by, I had a clean path between it and the man. A direct target. I revved the engine once, then again. I put it in drive and took a deep breath before committing to the gas pedal. Why did the drunks get to live?

Rocks upended against my car. Stan shouted, *Serena, don't!* But I was already in motion, preparing to feel the crunch of bones between the two vehicles.

I smashed the brake a half second before contact. The man's glossy eyes stared back, and his head bounced against the dented metal of the car. Emergency lights sprayed behind him.

The man slurred, "I told you to wear that blasted belt."

Stan opened the truck's passenger door.

"Just ease it back, Serena. Put it in reverse and ease it back."

I shook my head *no.*

"Please, Serena."

"I want him to die!"

"I know you do."

"We were wrong, Stan."

"We couldn't have known."

"Why? Why does he get to live?"

"He'll have to live with what he did."

"The pain," I cried. "It's too much. It's too much, Stan."

"I know, Serena," he said. "We'll bear it together."

A CHP cruiser whipped to the scene and angled between the other cars. In the moment of distraction, Stan jerked the keys from the ignition.

Tears flooded as I surrendered and put it in park, beating the steering wheel with my fist.

The stretch of Stockton Boulevard was closed for two hours as authorities worked the scene. Stan talked to them, telling them what we'd seen at the Midtown Farmers Market, how the man had abandoned his child at our stall. He didn't tell them the hurtful thing. That we'd watched him walk off drunk with the child. They covered June with a white sheet and carried her off. They cuffed the man and took him away, too. Stan, ever the one with solutions, asked if I still wanted to drive back. God love him, he was always prepared to let me go my own way.

"No," I told him. "You drive."

I once knew a woman who'd left on a vacation and asked her husband to water her favorite plant, which she'd left on the kitchen table. Easy to spot. When she returned, the plant was dead. He'd eaten right next to the dying thing for a week. Every time Stan did something sweet for me, I thought of how lucky I was to have a noticer.

I dug my nails into my hands, trying not to cry on the journey back home. But all I could picture was June's bright and hopeful face.

Thank you, Mims Peach People.

When we got to Oakdale, we had to go to Marge's house first and unload. There in the drive sat Marge and a huddle of the Oakdale wives. We got out of the truck, and they rose in unison.

"Stan sent a message," she said. "What can we do?"

"There's no need," I said, trying to wave them off. I went to the back of the truck, preparing to return Marge's things.

"You've had a shock, Serena," Marge said. "Shared pain is lessened, or don't I know it. We all do."

The women surrounded me.

"I can't sit. I can't sit in the circle," I said. "It's too much. I feel like the pain is exploding inside me, and I want to break something. I want to smash something into a million pieces."

Marge looked behind me and jutted her chin. Stan was unloaded the remaining peach crates. Marge bent for them and put a peach in my hand.

"Smash away."

"What?"

Marge curled another peach like a baseball pitcher and sent it into the side of her garage. It hit with impressive violence.

"Fuck cancer," she said.

Then she nodded at me.

I threw it. "Fuck drunks."

The anger in me swirled.

I gripped two more peaches and launched them in rapid succession. The fruit exploded. I threw three more, feeling the burn ripple through my arm, letting out some primal moan as I did.

We went through the entire crate, Marge and I. Forcing the peach flesh to suffer. Exhausting our fury, if only for a moment. Soon, the air was thick with peach scent and the distant sound of bleating sheep. The other women and Stan timidly moved closer. There were no words spoken.

Maybe there were no words for this kind of misery. We just had to stand in it for a while.

WINGING IT

Debra Henry

Zosia handed the man in the gray beanie an order of spicy apricot wings and coleslaw. "Can I get you anything else?"

He shook his head, paid his bill from a wad of cash wrapped with a rubber band, then sauntered from her food truck to one of the tables she'd set up in the shade of some nearby trees. People enjoyed the variety of chicken wings she served, so she parked near the Crocker Art Museum on Wednesdays, Thursdays and Fridays. She was close enough to Sacramento's Capitol Mall and Crocker Park that she drew a steady stream of customers to Winging It.

"What's that?" a freckle-faced teenager asked while she and her friend waited for their coconut curry wings and fries. She was pointing to a row of rubber chickens strung along the side of Zosia's white truck. Both girls giggled.

"My brother used them as gags ... to make people laugh," Zosia said, trying to smile as she set their order onto the counter at her serving window. She didn't add that her brother, Tomasz, had died well over a year ago. She clipped the rubber chickens to her truck in his memory.

The guy in the gray beanie, a scrawny Latino, was still at the table near the elm trees an hour after she'd served him, his wings and coleslaw long gone. Most customers finished eating in under fifteen minutes, but he was taking his own sweet time. She'd noticed people stop at his table, take a seat, and head off after a couple of minutes. Some suspicious transactions were going on, but Gray Beanie was covering it well. Zosia decided to investigate.

"You want something else to eat?" she asked after making her way to his table.

"Naw. Doin' just fine."

"My other customers might wanna sit down." Zosia pointed to two nearby tables, both occupied and to several customers leaning against trees and perched on the edge of a cement planter. She picked up Gray Beanie's empty cardboard serving tray and used napkin. "You sellin' something?" she asked.

He glared at her. "Ain't none of your business."

She held her ground and glared back. "Matter of fact, it is my business." She crumpled the cardboard tray. "That's *my* table you're sitting at, *my* chairs."

"You gonna' do somethin' bout it?"

"What you selling?" Zosia asked again.

The man took his time answering. "Jewelry," he finally said, wearing a smug smile. "My cousin who makes it don't work out'a no store. I'm the delivery guy. Deliver the goods and get the payment." He patted the black shoulder bag on the table.

Zosia considered this. "You're using my business to do your business? Seems like I should be getting a cut."

Grey Beanie scowled, but she kept a straight face.

"How about a pearl necklace, a jade bracelet, something?" She tried to look like she carried some authority. At five foot two it was hard to pull off.

"Listen up, lady. My cousin ain't gonna be happy you musclin' in on profits."

"Oh yah, then maybe you ought'a find somewhere else to do your business."

Zosia was in over her head, but it was hard to contain her anger. She'd moved to Sacramento with her brother Tomasz from Poland, hoping for a better life. He'd been helping put her through college when he died, so she'd dropped out and bought a used food truck with money she'd borrowed. Working six days a week, she was saving up to enroll in a culinary program in San Francisco. At the moment, though, she was barely breaking even, so school was out of the question. Unless she came into some kind of a windfall. And here was this pushy punk taking advantage of the business *she* was building.

"I'll tell you what," Gray Beanie said. "You cook me some of those green jalapeño wings. Consider me a brand-new customer. Give me another hour."

Zosia set her hands on her hips and gritted her teeth. "What's your name anyway? And who's this damned cousin of yours?"

"Just call me Ray, like ray of sunshine."

Zosia didn't like it but returned to the truck and fried up some wings. She bought the raw wings from her uncle who operated an organic poultry farm out near Herald. She was lucky, he gave them to her for next to nothing—said they were mostly waste to him. She knew better and appreciated his generosity.

When she'd finished filling the order for Mr. Sunshine, she added extra jalapeños and a dollop of hot sauce, causing her nose to tingle. Hopefully, the wings were so hot Ray would scorch his throat. She could call 911 and have an ambulance take him out of her hair.

"You here tomorrow?" Ray asked when she called out his order and he strolled over.

"Why? You bringing me a diamond ring?"

"My cousin gonna pay me a visit. You can ask for a diamond ring yourself." Ray paid for his order, returned to his place at her table and entertained company for the next half hour. When he finally stood and wandered off, Zosia breathed a little easier.

***

At seven-thirty, when business slowed and the air began to cool, Zosia closed her customer window, exhausted from having to stand and wear a smile all day. She hurried through her clean-up routine: emptying oil from the fryer, squeezing the sauces and condiments into the fridge where the unused wings and leftover food all vied for space. After wiping down the counters with disinfectant, she hauled the collapsible tables and fold-up chairs to the truck and maneuvered them inside. Last of all, she brought Tomasz's rubber chickens into the truck. Would she ever be able to accept his sudden and pointless death? He'd been working construction, building houses for the homeless, when he stopped into a corner store for a takeaway sandwich. He'd been killed in a robbery gone wrong. A feeling of weariness washed over her and her ribs felt too tight to contain the pain in her heart. A lump formed in her throat as she got behind the wheel and drove away.

***

The day didn't end when she arrived home. She added up her day's earnings, looked through her accounts for the past month and had some dinner: leftover salad and wings. Promoters of eating local in Sacramento used a slogan: from farm to fork. She served customers local food from her uncle's poultry farm, but she had no shortage of competition. Trying to make a living in the food industry was tough. Anyone who could fill a taco or flip a burger was competing for empty stomachs right alongside her.

While eating, Zosia considered Gray Beanie, Mr. Ray Sunshine. Would his boss really show up at her food truck tomorrow? Or was Ray bluffing? She didn't buy his story about selling jewelry. It didn't add up. Best guess? He was dealing drugs. So why had she set out to harass him? It was rage seeping out. Anger at people like Ray, who took advantage of others and didn't give a rat's ass about the havoc they left in their wake. It wasn't her job to take on drug dealers or organized crime, but she'd been furious watching Ray rake in money while selling drugs to addicts. Maybe she should just park somewhere else tomorrow. She could set up at Discovery Park where she usually sold her wings on Saturdays. By next Wednesday, Ray would've moved on and found somewhere else to push his poison.

The more she considered the situation, the more anxious she felt. She pictured Ray's boss showing up, a big thug with bulging biceps, imagining him pulling a gun and killing her because she'd poked her nose where it wasn't wanted. She'd end up dead like her brother. Tomasz had stepped in when the robber at the corner store pointed a gun at the owner. The owner survived, but Tomasz was shot in the chest and died in an ambulance on the way to the hospital.

Zosia climbed the stairs from her basement suite to say good night to her aunt and uncle. They were playing cards and asked about her day. She didn't mention her argument with a drug dealer.

"I'll have the boxes of wings you need for tomorrow ready by ten," her uncle said. "Sleep well."

"Thanks." Zosia's aunt and uncle had provided her and Tomasz a home when they arrived in Sacramento from Warsaw. Her uncle had done everything in his power to help them succeed, though he and her aunt were working seven days a week to make a living.

After returning to her rooms, Zosia couldn't let go of her thoughts about Mr. Sunshine. Or his boss. She decided to call Garland Williams. She'd gotten to know Garland after her brother's death. As a deputy sheriff who was first on the scene, he'd helped support her through the nightmare when Tomasz's killer was arrested, went to trial and was finally convicted of murder. Garland might have some thoughts about the predicament she'd put herself in, come up with some ideas on how she could avoid being a victim of violence, like Tomasz.

She picked up her cell and called his number.

***

Thursday dawned sunny, with a forecast of temperatures in the mid-nineties. Small mercies that people still enjoyed eating hot wings in summer.

After Zosia prepared her food, she chatted with her uncle, who loaded the boxed-up wings into her food truck. Nervous after her call to Garland and his suggestion that she go ahead and set up her truck as usual, she was dragging her feet.

"Be careful out there," her uncle said, as though he had some inkling that trouble lay ahead. She drove out of Herald and onto the 99 toward Sacramento with Garland's reassurance that 'everything'll be fine' running in a loop through her brain like a mantra.

When she pulled up and stopped her truck at her usual location, she scanned the area for signs of trouble. Walkers, runners, cyclists and kids on skateboards kept the sidewalks and grassy area near the Crocker Art Museum busy with possible customers. A few teenagers kicked a soccer ball off in the distance, their voices rising and falling as their game progressed. There was no sign of Ray.

By the time she opened the order window for business, anxiety was prickling at Zosia's body and sweat began to bead on her back. She attached the rubber chickens to the clips on the side of the truck, leaving one inside for good luck. Tomasz had always had her back while they were growing up, but he wouldn't be here today—if she needed help.

When lunchtime approached, business picked up. There was still no sign of Ray, though. Maybe she'd misinterpreted the whole situation. She kept her eyes peeled anyway. Between serving customers, she scanned the area for a cocky Latino.

Then she saw him, wearing his trademark gray beanie. He strolled toward her, hands in his hoodie pockets, black bag slung across his chest. She took a deep breath and tried not to panic.

"Hey lady, you're here," he said as he approached the customer window, looking twitchy. "You mean to kill me yesterday with those wings?"

She didn't like the sound of the word kill. "You ordered jalapeño pepper wings. What did you expect? You gonna get them hot."

Ray checked the menu posted on a hinged sign bolted to the truck. "How 'bout you get me some of those wings with cherry sauce ... nice and sweet. And I'll have a cola."

"What you got there?" She nodded toward the black bag. "Your merchandise?"

Ray shook his head. "No diamond rings for you today. But boss's planning to drop by. Maybe you wanna meet and state your case. Good luck with that one." He let out a crazy cackle.

"With all that cash you got stashed away, looks like you're rollin' in money. You make enough to share the profits."

"Mind your own business," he said and turned to scope the area. Was he suspicious? Worried? Or looking to see if anyone would notice if he pulled a gun and shot her.

She handed him his wings and drink and took the bills he handed over. "Keep the change," Ray said and cackled again.

A couple approached her truck just after he took a seat, drawing Zosia's focus away from the drug dealer. The guy, a clean-cut young man, and the woman, an attractive red-head, both ordered honey mustard wings with a side salad. The two acted like love birds as she handed them their order. They sat down at the table closest to her truck and began eating.

Zosia grew frustrated serving her customers while watching Ray serve his. Her nerves were on edge. Forty-five minutes passed with no sign of Ray's boss. Zosia realized the love birds were still seated at the table nearest her truck. They were scrolling through their phones when the guy stood, came over to her counter and ordered two cups of coffee. "How's it going?"

"Pretty well," Zosia lied.

He motioned his head toward Ray. "Looks like that guy's got a few friends."

She nodded. "You noticed?"

The guy paid, picked up the coffee and sat back down at his table. She heard his phone ring and he answered it.

A couple of minutes later, a hefty blond woman walked by Ray. She was carrying a large blue shoulder bag. After taking off her sunglasses, she said something to Ray, then checked her watch and surroundings as though looking for something or someone. Was she one of his customers? Instead of sitting down, the woman came over to the truck's serving window.

"Can you get me an order of fries," she said in a voice that seemed too high for someone with such a large build.

Zosia lowered a basket of frozen chips into the deep fryer and turned back to the woman.

"How long you been operating round here?" the woman asked.

"About a year."

"Business good?" The woman rummaged through her bag. "I bet you're makin' a good living."

Zosia wasn't going to admit she was barely breaking even. She liked her customers to think she was a successful entrepreneur.

"I'm saving up for culinary school. I wanna open my own restaurant."

"But I hear you been hasslin' my delivery guy," the woman said, lowering her voice. "You askin' for trouble?"

Zosia's throat tightened, making it almost impossible to talk. She'd never suspected Ray's boss would be a woman. And now here she was, face to face with a drug lord who probably wanted to kill her.

"No," she said, "I'm not looking for trouble. I just thought you two might want to team up. You could do your business here ... and at my other locations. I'd provide you and your customers with a table and chairs ... and cover." Zosia was lying. She had no intention of supporting a drug trafficker or organized crime.

The woman laughed. "You think I need you?" She reached into her bag again and pulled out a gun.

Zosia's stomach lurched. It was all she could do not to pass out. She thought about Tomasz, facing a desperate man who wanted money to feed his drug habit. The addict had turned to Tomasz when he'd tried to reason with him. It hadn't worked. The man shot him in cold blood and fled from the store without getting a dime.

Zosia gulped for air. "Listen," she croaked. "We can forget all about me getting a cut. It was just a stupid idea."

With her back to the boulevard and park, Blondie didn't see what was happening behind her. Garland Williams had materialized from out of nowhere and confronted Ray. Ray, abandoning his leather satchel, was now running toward the soccer players off in the distance. The lovebirds at their table were carefully watching what was happening at the customer window.

"Looks like your delivery guy decided to cut his losses," said Zosia.

When Blondie turned around to see what she was talking about, Zosia grabbed Tomasz's rubber chicken and belted her in the side of the head. Blondie caught off guard, lost her balance. At that moment, the lovebirds sprang from their chairs and pulled guns from holsters strapped under their shirts. Zosia picked up the gun Blondie had dropped onto the serving counter to take it out of the equation. There were far too many guns for comfort. Each of the undercover cops grabbed one of Blondie's arms. Zosia's hands were shaking as she set Blondie's gun back onto the counter.

"Thank God you're here," she said, her body sagging.

"We've got this now," the woman said. "You okay?"

"I guess." Zosia closed her eyes trying to blot out the image of Ray's boss pointing a gun at her.

"That rubber chicken came in handy," the man said as he handcuffed Zosia's would-be killer. Another officer led her away.

"I was just winging it," Zosia said, and she had been.

The female undercover cop shook her head and her partner smirked. "Speaking of wings, the ones we just ate were very tasty."

Zosia took the overcooked fries from the grease and set them aside. Her day of selling wings was probably over.

A crowd had gathered to witness the drug bust in progress. Zosia looked past them to Garland, still in a brawl with Ray Sunshine out in the field as another agent ran toward him. As she watched, the soccer team stopped their game. They circled Ray so Garland was able to take control of the situation.

While Zosia waited to be questioned, the number of uniformed officers grew, and a couple of media outlets showed up with microphones and cameras. It seemed like a circus as they took video footage of her truck and the activity involved in arresting Ray and his boss. Zosia learned from several of the officers that Blondie was Rita Ramirez, better known as The Needle, for how she was rumored to get rid of her competition. Apparently, she was a major player in drug smuggling and active in laundering money. Everyone seemed pleased to have her in custody.

After handing Ray over to the arrest team, Garland jogged toward her truck. "I told you I had your back," he said. "It was touch and go, though, when The Needle arrived. We hadn't expected such a big catch. You did good here."

"Tomasz would be happy one of his rubber chickens saved my life."

Garland laughed. "You did him proud."

"He was a hero," said Zosia.

"And so are you."

***

The Wednesday after the takedown, members of the Drug and Intelligence Division of the DEA gathered near the Crocker Art Museum to make a statement about the arrests of Rita Ramirez and Ray Gonzalez. Zosia's white food truck with the plastic rooster comb attached to its roof was visible in the background when officials involved in the press conference got started. After describing the sting operation that had taken place the previous Thursday, there were further remarks.

"A raid was made at the residence of one Rita Ramirez following her arrest," a man from the DEA said into a microphone. "We found dozens of guns, a stash of opioids and cash amounting to a quarter million dollars. A considerable number of deadly weapons have been taken out of circulation and a large quantity of drugs has been removed from our streets. All thanks to a citizen who alerted the sheriff's office to some suspicious activity and participated in our undercover operation."

Zosia, who was taking advantage of the crowd to sell some chicken wings, heard the applause for the successful drug bust. Calling Garland about Ray and his boss and agreeing to set up her truck so the drug squad could nab them had been her way of getting some payback for her brother's death. Somehow, the arrests didn't give her the satisfaction she hoped for. Tomasz was dead.

The press conference continued with questions, but Zosia stayed out of the limelight, selling chicken wings. Garland joined her at her truck.

"How you holding up?" he asked.

Zosia closed her eyes to consider. "Nothing'll bring Tomasz back," she said, her mouth dry.

"I know. But his killer's behind bars now, and you've helped take two drug dealers out of commission. That should mean something."

Zosia shrugged.

Garland pulled an envelope from a pocket inside his uniform jacket. "When Tomasz's killer was sentenced, you made a victim statement and filled out an application to Victim's Services. The Board has decided you deserve compensation for what happened to your brother."

He held out the envelope. "This is for you."

Zosia bit her lip.

"Come on, you deserve it," Garland said, so she took the envelope and opened it.

Reading the number on the check, she gasped. "Ten thousand dollars."

Garland nodded. "Tomasz was putting you through college when he died. You had to drop out. I hear you've been saving up for some kind of food program. This might help you enroll a little sooner."

"I was hoping for a windfall, but this..." Zosia stepped out from her truck and hugged Garland.

"It might not seem like justice, but there *are* good people in law enforcement and in the justice system." Garland nodded toward the press conference where the DEA was answering questions. "Like these people."

"You're right." she said. "People just like you."

FAIR AND FOWL

Nick Webster

I had never met Apollo Perry and assumed that his name was as make believe as his job title: pet detective. It was a Saturday around six a.m., and a group of us stood in a stuffy doublewide housed on the grounds of the county fair. It reminded me of the calm before a gunfight at a corral in an Internet streamed western. Apollo Perry held court. He was an odd-looking man, even for an odd time of the morning.

Earlier that morning, a customer of the insurance company I work for called about filing a claim. Mr. Brand—he insisted I call him this—had submitted a claim for two missing chickens. At my home office, in my boxers, I logged on to my computer and saw that Mr. Brand had purchased a life insurance policy for two breeder chickens. We were just waiting for a certificate of authenticity, whatever that was.

I was hesitant about calling my supervisor. But, I knew nothing about chickens or fowl and called anyway. This was at five a.m. on a Saturday morning. I was lucky to catch him on his way to a golf course.

"Apollo Perry is our animal expert," he said. "I'm counting on you. You might learn something valuable." I heard the metallic sound of clinking golf clubs in the background. "I'll be the new club record holder when we speak next," he said and hung up.

What was left unsaid was that I was still on probation, and my supervisor had just given me a negative evaluation and one more chance to improve. I couldn't blame him. I had trouble making sense of a recent romantic breakup, and confrontations became unbearable. My supervisor noticed.

After a few minutes of fat fingering Apollo Perry's name into my phone, I finally found his contact information and a photo. It showed a balding, heavyset deputy holding an award plaque.

I called him. A crisp, efficient voice answered. "Perry."

I introduced myself and explained the situation.

"Interesting. Meet me at the fairgrounds at six a.m. sharp and make sure Mr. Brand is there."

I called Mr. Brand to arrange for him to meet me and Apollo Perry.

"Great," Mr. Brand said. "I'm bringing the livestock supervisor. Let's meet at his office." He hung up abruptly, and I dressed and drove to the fairgrounds.

Walking to the livestock supervisor's doublewide in a pair of loafers, I took in the sights. This May morning in Sacramento was cool; a soft light coated the fairgrounds like silk. In the distance was the midway, with a three-story wheel shining in the center. Next to the midway were the livestock barns. The barns, teamed with a variety of earnest 4-H members, put-out FFA high schoolers and their frazzled parents. An odor, likely the mix of pig feces and urine-soaked straw, wafted to the parking lot.

The doublewide was easy to find, and I crept up three creaky wooden stairs to reach a deck and entered through the door. The inside featured wood paneling, a dim overhead light, and a metal desk. Two men stood opposite from Apollo Perry.

When I entered, Mr. Brand looked at me and said: "You must be the guy with the checkbook." He was an average-looking suburban dad with a weak chin and large eyes that appeared exhausted, likely having not slept in twenty-four hours. His hair, which was shaped like a bird's nest, made him look even more desperate.

"We'll see," I said. Mr. Brand handed me a document entitled "Certificate of Authenticity." I folded the document and put it in my back pocket.

"Everybody, take a seat. Let's get started." This was the livestock supervisor, Bo Cameron, an older man with a white pencil mustache who wore a cowboy shirt, jeans, and boots. Bo had a cowboy hat in his gnarled hand that he put on his knee when he sat on a folding chair. A Styrofoam cup seemed glued to his right hand, and he raised this cup to his mouth every few minutes and spit. It was a natural pose for him.

"All we need is for my insurance guy to verify my claim," Mr. Brand said. "Then we can get out of here."

"It's like I told you over the phone. Mr. Perry..."

Apollo cleared his throat and said: "Apollo will do."

"Apollo," I continued, "was hired by the insurance company to verify the claim."

"Isn't that what I pay you for?" Mr. Brand said.

Just because he paid premiums didn't mean he paid me. I considered my supervisor's admonishment and let it go. "I have no expertise in assessing poultry. My supervisor recommended Mr..."

Apollo looked at me, ready to preempt.

"Apollo," I continued, "to review the evidence and provide me an assessment so I can validate or deny the claim."

Mr. Brand pursed his lips, he shook his head and looked at Apollo, sizing him up. "You're the expert?"

"My resume includes twenty-five years as a detective with the county sheriff's office. I retired and for the last five years have investigated pet disappearances, wrongful deaths, and the like."

Mr. Brand folded his arms across his chest. "You're a pet detective?"

Bo snorted and chuckled. "Come again?" he asked and spit into the cup. "That sounds made up."

Mr. Brand looked at me. "My daughter stands to lose a lot of money, and you bring a pet detective?"

Before I could respond, Apollo said: "Investigations are the same, whether they are people or animals. Evidence, deduction, conclusions." He pointed at me and said: "In short, what makes me an expert is the insurance company says I am."

Appearing to give up, Bo exhaled, tossed his hat on a desk, and leaned forward. "What's next?" he asked and spit. "The fair board doesn't want a scandal."

"Do you want to see the coop?" This was Mr. Brand. "There was a ransom note too."

"I'll get to that. When was the last time you saw the chickens?"

"Around ten o'clock last night. "My wife and I had drinks with the Klingmans near the midway and checked on the chickens before heading to our motorhomes."

"Your motorhomes are on the premises?"

"Livestock folks are here for four or five days," Bo said. "Some families bring an RV. There's a lot of hurry up and wait between showing animals and cleaning pens."

"Any ideas on who would want to steal your chickens?"

"It's probably a prank. It happens at least once a year."

"These are grand champion chickens. They'll command a high price at Sunday's livestock auction," Mr. Brand said.

"How much?"

"Last year's grand champion pen sold for seven grand," Bo replied.

"Let's assume that it's not a prank," Apollo said and looked at Mr. Brand. "Continue, please."

Mr. Brand looked at the ceiling. "The only people I can think of are—I hate to say it—the Klingmans."

"Who are the Klingmans?"

"Their daughter's chickens were the reserve grand champions," Bo said.

"The two of you are friends?" Apollo asked.

"For ten years," Mr. Brand said and sank into his seat. "My wife—she's in the Exhibition Hall as a calligrapher—would be devastated. Do you want to meet her?"

"Eventually, yes. For now, can I meet the Klingmans?"

"They are likely at the barns. I can introduce you." Bo said.

Apollo nodded and stood up. I was surprised at how short and heavy he was. On his balding head, he put a straw-braid, pork pie hat with a feather stuck neatly into the brim and walked outside.

The three of us followed. Apollo paused until we caught up. "Will you take me to the poultry area?" he asked when Bo approached.

With a limp, Bo took the lead and walked us through the barns.

Trying to keep up with Apollo, Bo said: "The Klingmans have been coming to this fair for three generations. The grandfather is my age. Always had one scheme or another. My guess is that the father is not much different. The Brands are new to poultry."

"Yet their pen won grand champion?" Apollo said.

Bo spit. "Beginners luck."

Apollo hopped over a cow pie and dodged a steer being walked through the barn by a junior high 4-Her. I kicked dust and straw off my loafers.

"Why weren't the chickens stolen on Thursday?" Apollo asked.

Bo continued. "The grand champion is awarded on Thursday. All market poultry is required to take part in showmanship on Friday, to qualify for the auction on Sunday. Here it is."

We stopped in front of a row of coops that rested waist-high on tabletops. I had stepped in chicken shit and wiped the white and green mess in the wood chips. Apollo looked at my loafers and then went back to inspect the pens. The air was grimy with a variety of barnyard smells and particulate matter. I heard a rooster crowing somewhere. Hens clucked in their pens.

"It's the empty coop, near the middle." This was Mr. Brand, who stood beside Bo. Apollo, his hands behind his back, leaned over and walked along the row of pens then double backed on the other side. He paused at the empty coop and looked inside.

"What was the status of the door?"

"Status?" Mr. Brand asked.

Bo spit. "I think Apollo means was the door open, shut, locked, unlocked."

"Correct," Apollo said.

Mr. Brand ran a hand through his unkempt hair. "Why does it matter?"

I wondered about Mr. Brand's evasion. Before I could answer, Apollo said: "It's possible the door was left open or wasn't locked, and the chicken hopped out and ran away. It would be negligence on the caretaker."

"And I couldn't validate the claim," I added. A reminder that I had a role in this investigation seemed appropriate, but Apollo looked at me like I had farted into a windsock. I went into listen-only mode.

"I don't remember," Mr. Brand said. "It was dark. I panicked."

"You said there was a ransom note?"

"There was."

"Was?" Bo asked.

"It was an e-mail that was recalled before I could save it."

Apollo's facial expression didn't change. He continued looking closely at the empty cage, pinched and shook the tines. "Do you remember what the e-mail said?"

"All I could see was the subject line and the first line: Trouble, Your chickens are in our possession. You have…"

"You're sure that's all the e-mail said?" This was Bo, who was changing out his dip. He tossed the yellow remains on the dirt floor and pushed another finger full in his mouth.

Mr. Brand nodded.

Apollo wiped his hands on a handkerchief he had removed from his back pocket and joined our group. "The pen appears unmolested, so there was no forced exit or entry."

"We should start phoning local poultry farms and see if they've been approached about a sale," Mr. Brand said.

"That won't be necessary," Apollo said.

"Why?"

Apollo folded the handkerchief and slid it into his back pocket. "The chickens are still on fairground property."

Bo spit and moved through the group, limping toward a husband and wife walking through the barn. I couldn't understand what was said but was led to believe they were the Klingmans. They were one of those attractive, confident couples who looked at home anywhere.

Bo came back and said to Mr. Brand: "I told them the same thing I told you. Your pet detective must find the chickens by noon or we're giving Klingman the top spot." Mr. Brand's face paled as he nodded.

Bo walked back to Apollo and me. "Did you hear that? Noon."

It didn't matter to me what was sold at auction. I was there to validate a claim, so I said: "I heard you."

Apollo just grunted.

"Do you want to speak to the Klingmans?" Bo asked.

"Of course," Apollo said.

"Now's your chance. I'll keep Mr. Brand from interfering."

"Brand!" This was Klingman. He waved and said: "I'm sorry about your pen."

"Thanks," Mr. Brand said and walked away from the pens with Bo. It was awkward, and I was glad to follow Apollo to where the Klingmans stood.

The Klingmans looked like local celebrities. Each wore cowboy boots, long-sleeve plaid shirts with pearlized snaps, and pressed blue jeans. Their smiles were infectious, as were the unassuming looks in their eyes. I felt right away that the Klingmans didn't steal the chickens. They didn't need to.

I explained my role and introduced Apollo. The Klingmans didn't smirk when I said Apollo was a pet detective. "Nice to meet you," both said with welcoming smiles.

If the couple's charisma overpowered Apollo, he didn't show it. "Mr. and Mrs. Klingman, how would you characterize your relationship with the Brands?"

The smiles faded. The Klingmans looked at each other. "Solid. Fun," Mrs. Klingman said.

"Where were you last night?"

"Drinks and dinner on the midway." This was Mr. Klingman.

"It was a celebration," Mrs. Klingman said. She twisted her hands. "Our daughters had won the top awards for market poultry."

"What time were you in the barns last night?"

"We walked through to get to our RV," Mrs. Klingman said. "Around ten o'clock."

"Was Mr. Brand with you?"

"No," Mr. Klingman said. "He didn't want to go to bed yet. He stood just outside the barns on the midway side and stretched his legs."

"Does he do this normally?"

"By golly, it was odd," Mrs. Klingman said. "He seemed to watch us walk."

"That's true," Mr. Klingman said. "He was still standing there when we reached the other side of the barn."

"With the other pen of chickens missing, your daughter's chickens will be first in line at the auction," I said.

Mr. Klingman rubbed the back of his neck and didn't respond.

"Bo said that Brand had until noon," Mrs. Klingman said.

"What does that mean, exactly?" This was Apollo.

The couple looked at each other. Mrs. Klingman squeezed her husband's hand.

"A better auction price for my daughter's pen," Mr. Klingman said. He appeared to be on the verge of tears. "She has worked so hard. Sorry," he said and covered his eyes with a hand.

"We're not without means," Mrs. Klingman said, rubbing her husband's back. "But, the extra money will help fund our daughter's college tuition next year."

I had been let into the Klingman's world. Seeing these two beautiful people stumble and hold each other up, I wanted to cut a check for the daughter's tuition right then, even if it would need a bank overdraft and a credit card to cover.

"Is there anything else that might help me?" Apollo asked.

"Talk to the vet, Dr. Newcome," Mrs. Klingman said and pointed to what looked like an information booth a few rows over. "There was an incident yesterday during the health check in."

"Why can't you tell us?" I asked.

"Even in the chicken barns, it better to get it from the horse's mouth," Mrs. Klingman said.

Apollo thanked the couple for their time and proceeded to the information booth. I didn't want to leave these charming people but thought about my supervisor and followed Apollo.

The booth was a poultry health station. I knew this because hanging behind a table was a black velvet poster that read "Poultry Health Station" with a rooster stitched into the corner. A man who looked like a tall, skinny cyclist with a streamlined nose, bright eyes, and a balding head sat behind a table, scrolling on his phone. The white lab coat made him look like a doctor on television. I was half right.

"I'm the veterinarian," Dr. Newcome said. "It's my first time."

Apollo appeared to have introduced himself.

"Can you describe your interactions with Mr. Brand?" This was Apollo.

"Brand?" he said and looked like he was choosing his words. "He's new to poultry."

"How does that make him different from most of the other entrants?"

Newcome exhaled and said: "It'll take a bit to explain." To me, he seemed put out.

Apollo didn't notice. "We have all day until noon."

"Chickens are market or breeder," Newcome said. "They had different weigh-in times on Thursday. Market weigh-in was first, breeder weigh-in second. Mr. Brand showed up at the end of the market weigh-in. Do you know why?"

"I hope at some point you'll tell me," Apollo said. "Like I said..."

"All day, until noon, got it," Dr. Newcome said. "Mr. Brand spent an hour, while I'm conducting health checks on other poultry entrants, trying to get me to sign a certificate of authenticity."

"What's that?" I asked.

"Basically, it says that a chicken is purebred. Pure breeds get top dollar."

"Interesting," Apollo said.

I removed the certificate from my back pocket and gave it to Apollo who showed it to Newcome and asked: "Is this your signature?"

"Nope," he said. "I couldn't sign. There wasn't enough time to verify the pedigree."

Apollo returned the document to me. "I think that answers your question, young Robert."

"What do you mean?" This was Newcome.

I kicked wood shavings on the ground with my loafer and explained the purpose of my visit to the fairgrounds today and Apollo's role. The veterinarian laughed.

"Pet detective?" he asked. "That's the funniest thing I've ever heard.

Apollo turned to me. "The claim is predicated on a chicken being used as an asset that generates profit, correct?"

"Correct, he has a policy on two chickens," I replied. "Each chicken on the policy must be used for breeding before he could cite loss of revenue. It could be for any number of reasons. Chickens die or run away..."

"Or were stolen," Apollo said.

"Correct," I said.

"But because each chicken was going to auction, it wouldn't be an asset anymore."

"Which nullifies the policy and invalidates the claim," Apollo said.

Apollo thanked the vet for his help and walked out of the barns toward the midway. I folded the certificate and followed. The sounds and smells of the barns behind us, we passed under the shade of eucalyptus trees between a closed market and the Exhibition Hall when Apollo said: "His perfidy aside, you can tell Mr. Brand that he has no claim."

We passed into the sun and out of the shade. A large water pipe had broken in the middle of the night, and we walked around a large puddle of water that surrounded a grassy knoll.

We paused in front of a tofu food truck that was parked a foot from where the water was. It was ten a.m., and tofu appeared to be the only food on the midway for sale. Apollo adjusted the brim of his pork pie hat and read the menu.

"I'll let my supervisor know you performed your duties well," I said.

"Thank you," he said and watched my feet dance around a yellow blob on the ground then went back to reading the food truck menu.

"What's next for you?" I asked.

"I'm not done with this case," he replied. He stepped to the order counter and asked for a Sin Spicy and Lettuce Wrap combo. He paid and walked to me.

"Who signed the certificate of authenticity if the vet didn't," he said and picked up his order. "Plus, I intend to find those chickens."

"You only have two hours," I said.

Apollo ignored me and sat on a bench overlooking the puddle and ate his lettuce wrap. For a few minutes, I watched filling land on the front of his shirt then walked alone through the barn to find Mr. Brand. I wasn't looking forward to this confrontation and remembered my supervisor's guidance.

I found Mr. Brand inspecting his daughter's empty chicken coop. His hair still looked like a bird's nest.

He appeared desperate for clues and asked about the investigation.

"I'm sorry to report that you have no claim," I said.

Mr. Brand slammed the door on the chicken coop, the force of which just made the door open again. "How's that possible?" he asked.

"Your chickens were market chickens, not breeders. The policy covers breeders only.

"You saw the certificate of authenticity?" he asked. "Signed by a vet and everything."

I took out the document from my pocket and pointed to the signature block. "Dr. Newcome didn't sign this document."

He yelled at me now. "If he didn't, who did?"

"I don't know for certain, but a handwriting analysis would likely show who forged the signature on that document."

"Now, you're calling me a liar?" Mr. Brand said. Spittle had formed on the ends of his mouth. I lifted my hands to the height of my shoulders, palms up and backed away.

"It'll all be in my report," I said. "I just wanted to tell you in person."

I turned to walk away and saw Apollo approach with a woman. The woman had a wide face and a bob haircut and wore a floral blouse, pedal pushers, and open-toed sandals. A chicken struggled under each of their arms. They stopped at the pens, loaded the chickens into the coop, and shut the wire door. A high school girl, braces glistening in her mouth, ran up from the direction of the motorhome area. She hugged the woman and sobbed.

Apollo came up to me. Down feathers clung to the filling that stained his shirt. I was off balance. Between the reunion and threats, I didn't know what to think. Not paying the claim would thrill my supervisor. My job may be safe for a little longer.

"That is Mrs. Brand and her daughter, I assume." This was me.

"You would be right, young Robert," Apollo said. "Will you find the Klingmans and Mr. Cameron and tell them to meet here? Their participation is urgently required." As I walked away, Apollo whispered: "Don't let them know about the status of the chickens."

I did as he asked and returned to the coops. The daughter wasn't present. Apollo stood between the two couples. Nobody spoke, and even the Klingmans seemed cold. It broke my heart.

I saw Bo enter the barns and limp toward us. He moved slower than a sunset and eventually joined the group. He spit and said: "It's almost noon. Find anything?"

"I'd say they did." This was Mrs. Brand, and she glared at her husband. Her hands were balled into little fists. Mr. Brand looked at the ground, his hands in his pockets.

The awkwardness was too much. "Apollo Perry has gathered you all together to present his findings." I stepped away from the group, stood next to a chicken coop, and took out my notepad and golf pencil to take down the exchange.

"It's almost noon," Bo said and spit. "Can I tell the auctioneer which pen will be first?"

"He found my daughter's chickens." This was Mrs. Brand.

Bo may have swallowed his chew because his voice was barely audible when he said: "Come again?"

Apollo plucked a down feather from his shirt. "As I said earlier, finding animals is not different from finding people: evidence, deductions, and conclusions."

"And you've concluded what?" This was Mr. Brand.

"As far as the claim, I believe young Robert told you."

"That certificate is not forged," Mr. Brand said. "You can't prove that."

"Yes, he can," Mrs. Brand said and put her head in her hands. "I forged it."

Mr. Brand's shoulders slumped, and he didn't speak.

"So, fine, Brand doesn't have an insurance claim," Bo said and looked at me. "Good for you." He spit and said: "Did Brand steal his own chickens too?"

"You know the answer to that question," Apollo said.

Bo snorted, then laughed. "Me?"

"What happened to your leg?"

Bo squinted and spit. "What's my limp have to do with anything?"

"I'll come back to that," Apollo said. "I'll address the fraud first and the theft second. Mr. Brand wanted to double his money and concocted a scheme where he could collect the life insurance money from young Robert's employer and sell a market chicken to a less discriminating buyer. When Dr. Newcome wouldn't sign the certificate, Mr. Brand asked his wife, who is a great calligrapher, to sign for Dr. Newcome."

"I told you it wouldn't work," Mrs. Brand yelled and punched her husband's shoulder. He didn't move or speak.

"If the claim is invalid, that doesn't mean that your daughter loses her spot," I said. "Does it?"

"It should." This was Mr. Klingman. "She shouldn't be able to sell at auction."

"Our daughter deserves the first spot," Mrs. Klingman said.

"I'll get to that," Apollo said. "So that on its own makes the claim invalid. Which takes me to the missing chickens."

"About time," Bo said.

"It would have taken a person who knew both the Brands and the Klingmans. A person who knew the fairgrounds well. And had twenty-four-hour access to the barns and knew the security measures."

"That sounds like Bo," Mr. Klingman said.

"Why do I need to steal a chicken?"

"Where were you at 1 a.m.?"

"In bed, asleep."

"You sleep at the fairgrounds?"

"Yes, this time of year."

"And who was with you?"

"I was by myself."

"Bo knows that the tofu food truck rarely gets customers and has trouble even keeping his business at the fair. The operator was only happy to help because Bo paid the vendor to house the chickens until noon."

"That sounds hard to believe," Mr. Klingman said.

"It's true," Mrs. Brand said. "I heard the tofu truck guy tell Apollo."

"I suppose this food truck guy had a receipt for the money I supposedly paid him?" Bo removed a finger full of old yellow tobacco with his gnarled hand and threw it on the ground.

"No, he didn't," Apollo said. "He had this." Apollo held up a clear plastic bag. Inside the bag was a flattened yellow ball of something.

"What's that?" Mr. Brand said.

"Chewing tobacco. It's the same color as the tobacco that Mr. Cameron spits."

Everybody, except Bo and Apollo, looked at the bag and the yellow smudge on the ground. Bo refilled his lip and spit.

"By golly, they are the same," Mrs. Klingman said.

Mr. Brand looked at Bo and asked: "Why'd you do it?"

"He didn't like Klingman and wanted to tarnish their image by making it appear they stole the chickens to get a better spot for their daughter."

"What about me?" Mr. Brand asked.

"You are new to poultry, and he didn't think your daughter earned the right to be grand champion," Apollo said.

"Beginner's luck," Bo said and spit. "All of that is fine for a story, Mr. Perry, but you can't prove any of it." Bo spit and started limping away.

"It's Apollo. What happened to your leg?"

"I don't owe an explanation to a pet detective," Bo said.

"You tripped over a concrete berm that was underwater when a pipe burst and hit your kneecap on the berm when you fell."

"It doesn't matter. The Klingman girl will go first."

I honestly thought Bo would get away with it when I heard: "No she won't."

A man the size of a football center with huge hands broke into our circle. He carried a walkie talkie that cracked and popped.

"This is the fair manager," Apollo said. He leaned closer to me and whispered. "I thought we'd need a little more firepower."

"Mr. Perry..."

Apollo cleared his throat.

"Sorry. Apollo filled me in. Mr. Brand, what you've done is criminal. You cannot take part in fair activities. You either Mrs. Brand."

"What about my daughter?"

"She did nothing wrong and keeps her awards and place at the auction."

"What about Bo?"

"I'll form a committee and see that he is punished," the fair manager said and leaned over to me. "The fair board doesn't want a scandal."

The group dispersed awkwardly. The Klingmans walked past the Brands who appeared to be in the middle of an argument. Apollo and I walked to the parking lot. Our cars happened to be near the same light pole.

"How did you know the chickens were still at the fairgrounds?" This was me.

He opened the door of his car, an old model Japanese sedan with oxidizing paint on the roof. "I've found that when the order of things is upset, it's the people closest to the disturbance who are the most responsible. Put simply, it's always somebody you know."

We got into our respective cars. I rode home and called my supervisor. He was still in the clubhouse, celebrating. I could smell the cigar smoke and cognac over the phone. "I trounced that record," he said.

He congratulated me on the investigation and asked what I learned.

"Fair is foul, and fowl is fair," I said.

About the Contributors

William Bishop was born and raised in Eureka, CA. He has a BA in French, BS in Computer Science, and a thirty-five year career as a machine designer. His interests are in linguistics (French, Spanish, Italian, Russian and Ukrainian), robotics, and philosophy. He is retired and currently lives in Modesto, CA. He now indulges in photography, chocolate candy making, playing classical piano, and writing. "Death of an Ugly Woman" is the second story he has published.

Sarah Bresniker is a mystery writer and former librarian who lives in Northern California. Her Arlie Wynne stories are fun, light mysteries revolving around the definitely made-up Ocean Grove Public Library where reference questions often involve murder, and the librarians have skills far beyond making book recommendations. She has published two short stories, one in the 2021 Sisters in Crime Guppy Anthology *The Fish That Got Away* and one in the 2023 Sisters in Crime San Diego Chapter Anthology *Crime Under The Sun*. She is working on her first novel, which was a finalist for the Claymore Award for unpublished manuscripts at Killer Nashville 2023. Learn more at SarahBresniker.com.

Chris Dreith got hooked on writing mysteries while creating plays for her local Carnegie Library's fundraiser, Mystery in the Library. While running her design/remodel business, she wrote several short stories, including "Old Soles" in the Bouchercon 2020 anthology, "Unknown Male and Parts of Two Others" in *Cemetery Plots of Northern California,* the Capitol Crimes 2021 anthology and "The Road To Limerick" in *Mystery Most International,* presented by the Mystery Patrons. Recently retired, she is happily adding more quirky short stories to her arsenal and working on her first thriller novel.

Susan Egan is a retired government lawyer who worked for two federal agencies for over thirty years in New York City. Her first love, and major in college, was Latin. She is a longtime mystery fan but also loves reading classical retellings, as well as epics in translation. When not reading or writing, Susan can be found in one of several places: at the ballet, at a museum, or in the Pilates studio. Susan also has three cats with literary names: Tristan from *Tristan and Isolde,* Hazel from *The Fault in Our Stars,* and Jane as in Eyre.

Elaine Faber is a member of Sisters in Crime, Northern California Publishers and Authors, and Elk Grove Writers Guild. She has published eleven cozy mystery novels, including a humorous historical fiction series, a cozy cat mystery series, an anthology of short cat stories, and multiple short stories in twenty-one independent anthologies. Three of Elaine's novels have won book awards through NCPA, as well as Excellence in Writing Certificates from Cat Writers Association. Elaine volunteers at the American Cancer Society Discovery Shop in Elk Grove, CA. She lives with her husband and Truffie, who contributes inspiration for her Black Cat Mysteries and multiple short stories. Elaine is available for speaking engagements or to mentor, beta read, or edit other authors' manuscripts.

Karen Harrington is a freelance writer and author from Texas. Her short work has appeared in *Shotgun Honey, Mystery Tribune, Alfred Hitchcock's Mystery Magazine,* and *Ellery Queen Mystery Magazine,* where she won the 2021 Ellery Queen Mystery Magazine Readers Choice Award for her short story "Boo Radley College Prep." She is the author of four novels, including *Sure Signs of Crazy* (Little, Brown, 2013), which has been translated into four languages and was a Kirkus Best Book of the Year. "The Strange Disappearance of Jason Whetstone," first published in the Sisters in Crime North Dallas anthology *Reckless in Texas*, appears in Best American Mystery & Suspense 2024. Learn more at KarenHarringtonBooks.com.

Debra Henry is a retired anthropologist and educator. An award-winning author whose short literary fiction is published in journals such as *Island Writer* magazine. Her short mysteries appear in *Crime Wave 1* and *Crime Wave 2*, anthologies published by Sisters in Crime Canada West.

Debra's short stories have won prizes several years running in the Victoria Writers' Society annual fiction and creative non-fiction writing contests. She is currently working on a police procedural novel, *Hooked on Murder*, set on northern Vancouver Island. Her short story, "Local Intelligence," included in *Crime Wave*, features the same characters and setting as her novel.

A member of the Victoria Writers' Society, Sisters in Crime, the Federation of BC Writers and Crime Writers of Canada, Debra lives in beautiful Sidney by the Sea on Canada's west coast with her husband and labradoodle, Quinn.

Virginia V. Kidd is a writer who lives in Sacramento, California, just a block and a half from an 80-year-old library. Like her character Mollie Walker, Virginia grew up on the Gulf Coast of Texas. She always loved learning, and she earned degrees from colleges in three parts of the U.S., including a B.A. from the University of Texas at Austin, an M.A. from California State University, Sacramento and a Ph.D. from the University of Minnesota

She taught Communication Studies for over three decades at California State University, Sacramento and was honored to be named an outstanding teacher in Arts and Letters in 2003. She is now an emeritus professor.

She has four cats: Trixie Beldon, Hardy, Black Bart, and Honey West. Two came as kittens from a rescue site. Two others just wandered up and decided to stay.

Karen A Phillips lives in northern California and has many short stories published in various anthologies. Her characters are engaging and fearless. She writes the Rocky Nelson Boxing Mystery series ... and yes, she does take boxing lessons. Visit her at KarenAPhillips.com.

Brian Shea once lived in the lower Sierra foothills where, through the generosity of a fifth generation rancher and his "ditch water" (irrigation allotment), he tilled and toiled on two acres of ranchland to demonstrate sustainable farming practices. He has sat at Slow Food feasts from California to Florida, supported MALT (Marin Agricultural Land Trust) and for several years was an art director for The Nature Conservancy.

Brian's story "Cavalry on Wings" appears in the 2024 anthology, *Invasive Species.* A second story, "Persimmon Constellation" is included in the 2024 Redwood Writers anthology, *Transitions.* He splits his time between designing books and writing a political thriller in which he kills yet another character.

Linda Joy Singleton wrote her first story when she was seven, dreaming of being a published author—and that dream came true! Now she's the author of over fifty-five books for children, including picture books and mystery series *Curious Cat Spy Club, Haunted Holidays, The Seer,* and *Dead Girl Walking.* She also collects vintage juvenile series; creating a home library of over 5,000 books. A longtime member of Sisters in Crime, she enjoys speaking at schools, libraries and conferences. She lives in the Northern California foothills, surrounded by a menagerie of animals including dogs, cats, peacocks, guinea hens, mini cows, horses and pigs. Book news, educational activities, and free stories are available at LindaJoySingleton.com.

Darrell Vaughn Smith has worked three decades as a reporter, editor and columnist for newspapers in California and Colorado and is a staff writer at The Sacramento Bee. His unpublished story "Kammerer Road" was named Best Short Story at the Elk Grove Great Read Book Fair. "Starkrimson" is his Capitol Crimes debut. He is married to education journalist Diana Lambert and the two live in Elk Grove.

Joanna Vander Vlugt is an author and illustrator. As a teenager, she drew charcoal portraits and wrote mysteries. Now, she uses Copic markers to illustrate motorcycles and graphic novels. Under the pseudonym J.C. Szasz, Joanna's short mysteries "Egyptian Queen," and "The Parrot and Wild Mushroom Stuffing" were both published in Crime Writers of Canada mystery anthologies. Her essay, "No Beatles Reunion" was published in the *Dropped Threads 3: Beyond the Small Circle* anthology.

Joanna draws upon her 13 years' experience working in the prosecutor's office and 10 years working in the Office of the Police Complaint Commissioner for inspiration for her novels. Joanna is the VP of Memberships for Sisters in Crime-CW. Joanna has just released her novel, *Spy Girls,* the third in her Jade & Sage series. Joanna's novels, art and podcast can be found at JoannaVanderVlugt.com

Nick Webster writes about do-gooders who accidentally operate on the margins of the law. He is the author of the Nate Salles detective series and the upcoming Gerald Raff crime series. He has held various jobs, including working in a print center, a pizza joint, and a bookstore, as well as counting cans of cat food in Carson City and managing sales proposals for Fortune 500 companies. He lives with his wife in Northern California. Learn more about him at AuthorNickWebster.com.

Dänna Wilberg – "The best secrets are the most twisted." Sarah Shepard's quote best describes author Dänna Wilberg's quest to unravel life's mysteries with every keystroke, on every page. Her series, *The Red Chair, The Grey Door,* and *The Black Dress,* featuring psychotherapist Grace Simms, pose the question: "What do we really know about a person?"

Dänna's paranormal Borrowed Time series about a woman who acquires a psychic gift after a near-death experience draws from her own experience producing/hosting the TV show "Paranormal Connection." Her plot points are ripped from the headlines, addressing issues such as serial murders, human trafficking, AI mind control, and cartels. Wilberg's characters are richly drawn and authentic, her scene settings span the globe, and her background as an award-winning script writer and filmmaker add magic to her storytelling. Her short films have won numerous awards, and her short stories can be found in anthologies world-wide. DannaWilberg.com

Tori Eldridge is the national bestselling author of the Lily Wong mystery thriller series, a two-time Anthony Award nominee, Lefty and Macavity Awards finalist, and winner of the 2021 Crimson Scribe Award for Best Book of the Year. Tori's Brazilian dark fantasy thriller, *Dance Among The Flames,* was inspired by her Academy Nicholl Fellowship semi-finalist screenplay, *The Gift*. Her shorter works appear in numerous anthologies, including *Back In Black, Crime Hits Home,* and *Weird Tales Magazine*. Tori kicks off her Ranger Makalani Pahukula Mystery Series with *Kaua'i Storm,* coming from Thomas & Mercer, May 20, 2025.

Before writing, Tori performed as an actress, singer, dancer on Broadway, television, and film in such shows as the original first national company of *Cats, The Love Boat,* and *Final Fantasy: The Spirits Within*. Born and raised in Honolulu—of Hawaiian, Chinese, Norwegian descent—Tori graduated from

Punahou School with classmate Barack Obama. She lives and writes from Portland, Oregon. Visit Tori at ToriEldridge.com.

Jennifer K. Morita is a former newspaper reporter, who juggled freelance jobs with being a stay-at-home mom for several years before becoming a writer for the communications department at a local university. Her first short story, "Cranes in the Cemetery" was published in the Capitol Crimes 2021 Anthology, *Cemetery Plots of Northern California*. In 2022 she was a runner up for the Sisters in Crime Eleanor Taylor Bland Award.

Her first novel *Ghosts of Waikīkī* will be released in November 2024 by Crooked Lane Books.

Jennifer is a past president of Capitol Crimes. Aside from leisurely hikes with her family, Zumba and Hot Hula are the only forms of exercise she willingly participates in. She lives in Northern California with her husband and two daughters. Visit Jennifer at JenniferKMorita.com

Acknowledgments

Our roots go back nearly thirty years to a pizza joint on Florin Road.

A handful of women met on a sunny October Saturday in 1995 and started Sacramento's chapter of Sisters in Crime, giving the California capital region a place for local writers to hone their craft and find support in the tough world of publishing. We owe Jacqueline Turner Banks, Pat Canterbury, Terri McMahon, Gabrielle Guedet, and Geri Spencer Hunter our deepest gratitude, because today Capitol Crimes is a flourishing community of 120 readers and writers from Sacramento and beyond, making it one of SinC's largest and most active chapters.

Farm to Foul Play marks Capitol Crimes' fifth short story anthology. The fifteen stories in this collection are a testament to our talented members as well as the bountiful Sacramento region and its rich agricultural history.

We are so grateful to our judges, Vinnie Hansen, Christina Hoag, Smita Harish Jain, Gary Phillips, and Kelli Stanley, who volunteered their time to read twenty-nine stories and shared their expertise in selecting the winning authors. A heartfelt thank you also goes out to Holly West, for her guidance and assistance with accepting submissions to ensure anonymity and a fair selection process.

Thank you to the 2024 Capitol Crimes Board including, President Claire Booth, Vice President Karen A. Phillips,

Secretary Jessica Cline, Treasurer James L'Etoile and members Paula Benson, Chris Dreith, Myra Jolivet and Richard Meredith for their unwavering support.

The Anthology Committee took on this daunting project more than a year before publication. Its first task was to select a theme. "How about 'Farm to Foul Play?'" Jessica Cline said over Zoom. She rattled off several more ideas, but the first one stuck. We tested it out with other members to be sure, and even at the Great Valley Bookfest panel in Manteca a month later. "That's perfect for Sacramento," said a woman in the audience.

And so it was.

Each committee member contributed her own unique talents to this anthology, whether it was Jessica's wise suggestions, Karen Phillips' beautiful cover, the keen marketing skills of Chris Dreith and Myra Jolivet, or Harriet Fox's unflagging smile and eagerness to help.

And finally, thank you to the members of Capitol Crimes for being such a supportive community for writers to flourish.

It has been a pleasure and honor to be part of the 2024 Capitol Crimes Anthology *Farm to Foul Play.*

Jennifer K. Morita
Capitol Crimes President Emeritus

If you enjoyed the stories in this anthology, please leave an honest review. Reviews sell more books and the revenue helps our mission to educate and support those who enjoy reading and writing crime fiction.
—*Capitol Crimes*

SPY GIRLS
A Jade & Sage Thriller Series
JOANNA VANDER VLUGT

Sheriff Bet Rivers is Back
A SHERIFF BET RIVERS MYSTERY
A COLD, COLD WORLD
ELENA TAYLOR
"Riveting"
Library Journal starred review
"Smart, action-packed suspense."
Lisa Gardner
#1 NYT Bestselling author
ALL WE BURIED
"A steller mystery."
Allen Eskens
USA Today Bestselling Author
www.ElenaTaylorAuthor.com

NIEA
FINALIST
A FINA MENDOZA MYSTERY
Welcome to Washington Fina Mendoza
KITTY FELDE
booklife
PRIZE
quarter finalist
"The West Wing" meets Nancy Drew

Black Cat Editing
Editing/Publication Services & From Plot to Print Course
Contact blackcatediting17@gmail.com
or visit blackcatediting.weebly.com

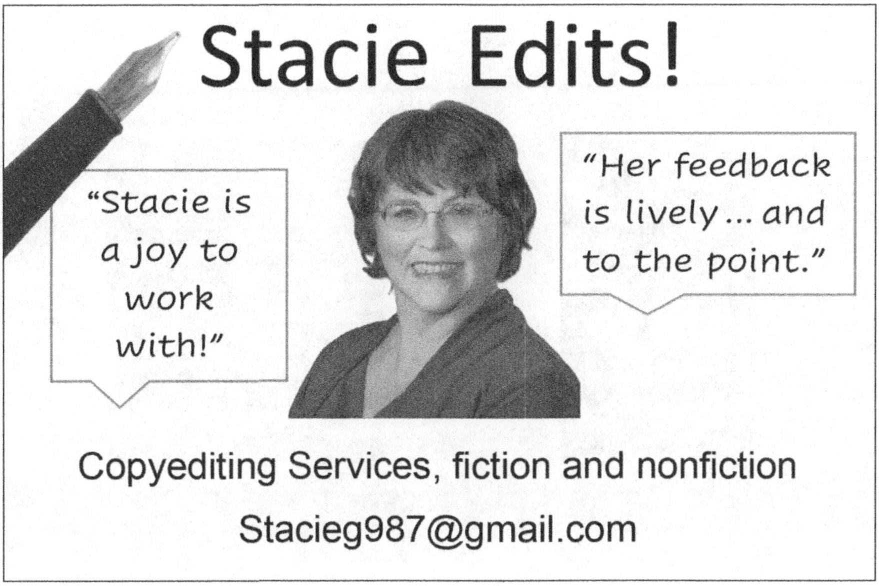
Stacie Edits!
"Stacie is a joy to work with!"
"Her feedback is lively… and to the point."
Copyediting Services, fiction and nonfiction
Stacieg987@gmail.com

Crow & Quoin
BOOK DESIGN
brianwrit@gmail.com

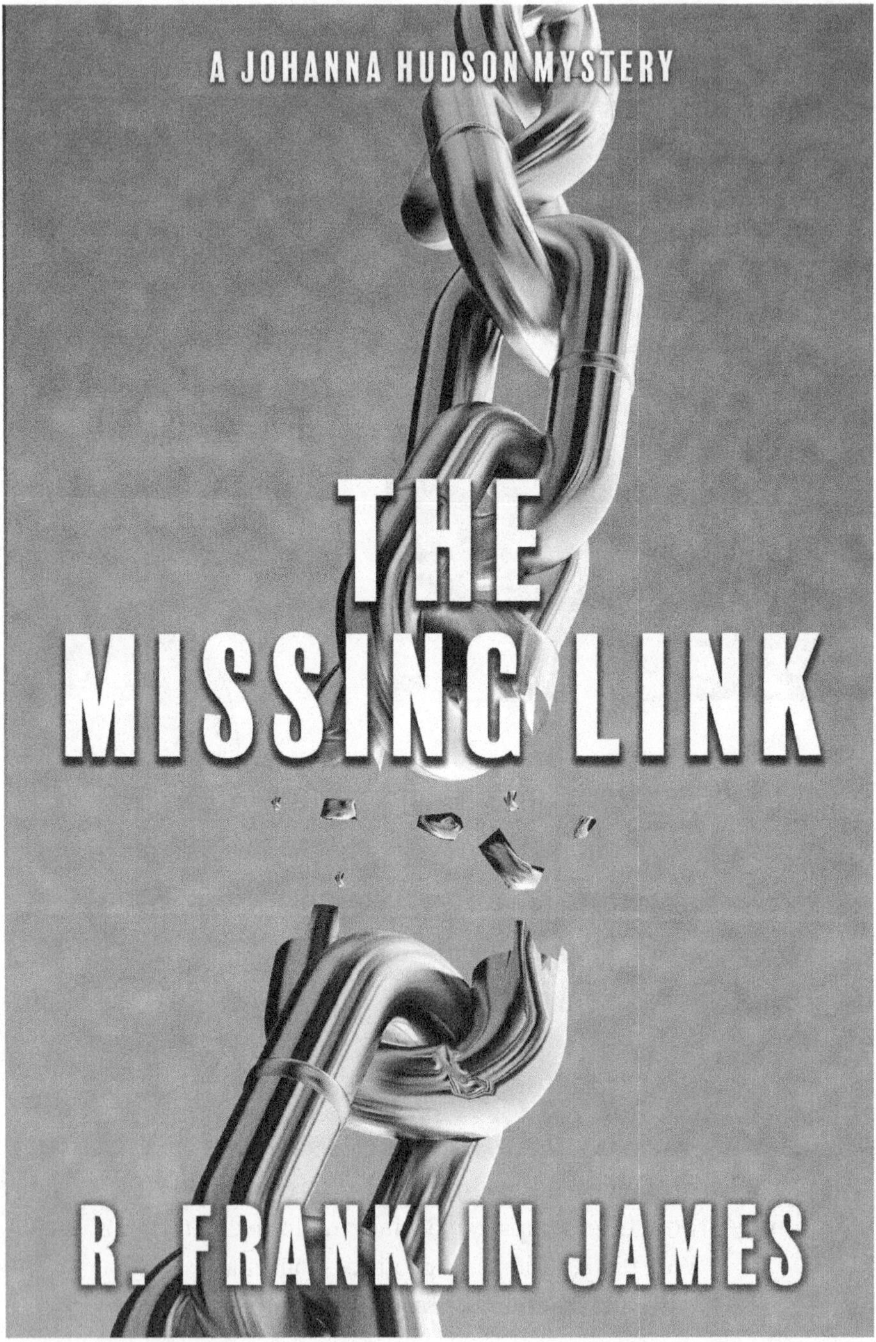
A JOHANNA HUDSON MYSTERY
THE MISSING LINK
R. FRANKLIN JAMES

Made in the USA
Las Vegas, NV
29 March 2026

44495828R00132